MEMOIRS FOUND IN A BATHTUB

STANISŁAW LEM
MEMOIRS FOUND IN A BATHTUB

Translated by
MICHAEL KANDEL and CHRISTINE ROSE

A Continuum Book
THE SEABURY PRESS
New York

First American Edition

Original edition: *Pamietnik znaleziony w wannie,* published by Wydawnietwo Literackie, Cracow, 1971.

Work by Christine Rose by arrangement with Forrest J. Ackerman.

Library of Congress Cataloging in Publication Data

Lem, Stanisław.
    Memoirs found in a bathtub.

    Translation of Pamiętnik znaleziony w wannie.
    I. Title.
PZ3.L5395Me [PG7158.L39]   891.8'5'37   72–10586
ISBN 0–8164–9128–3

INTRODUCTION

"Notes from the Neogene" is unquestionably one of the most precious relics of Earth's ancient past, dating from the very close of the Prechaotic, that period of decline which directly preceded the Great Collapse. It is indeed a paradox that we know much more of the civilizations of the Early Neogene, the protocultures of Assyria, Egypt and Greece, than we do of the days of paleoatomics and rudimentary astrogation. While those archaic cultures left behind permanent monuments in bone, stone, slate and bronze, almost the only means of recording and preserving knowledge during the Middle and Late Neogene was a substance called papyr.

Papyr was whitish, flaccid, a derivative of cellulose, rolled out on cylinders and cut into rectangular sheets. Information of all kinds was impressed on it with a dark tint, after which the sheets were collated and sewn in a special way.

In order to understand what brought about the Great Collapse, that catastrophic event which in a matter of weeks totally demolished the cultural achievement of centuries, we must go back three thousand years. Metamnestics and data crystallization did not exist in those days. Papyr performed all the functions now served by our mnemonitrons and gnostors. True, there were the beginnings of artificial memory; but these were large, bulky machines, troublesome to operate and maintain, and used only in the most limited, narrow way. They were called "electronic brains," an exaggeration comprehensible only in the historical perspective, much like the boast of the builders of Asia Minor, that their sacred temple Baa-Bel was "sky-reaching."

No one knows exactly when and where the papyralysis

epidemic broke out. Most likely, it happened in the desert regions of a land called Ammer-Ka, where the first spaceport was built. The people of that time did not immediately realize the scope of the impending danger. And yet we cannot accept the harsh judgment delivered by so many subsequent historians, that these were a frivolous people. To be sure, papyr was not distinguished by its durability; but one should not hold a Prechaotic civilization responsible for failing to foresee the existence of the RV catalyst, also known as the Hartian Agent. The true properties of this agent, after all, were discovered only in the Galactic Period by one Prodoctor Six Folses, who established RV's origin as the third moon of Uranus. Unwittingly brought back to Earth by an early expedition (the eighth Malaldic, according to Prognostor Phaa-Vaak), the Hartian Agent set off a chain reaction and papyr disintegrated around the globe.

The details of the cataclysm are not known. According to verbal reports crystallized only in the Fourth Galactium, the focal points of the epidemic were enormous data storage centers called li-brees. The reaction was practically instantaneous. In place of those great treasuries, those reservoirs of society's memory, lay mounds of gray, powdery ash.

The Prechaotic scientists thought they were dealing with some papyrophagous microbe, and wasted valuable time in the attempt to isolate it. One can hardly deny the justice of Histognostor Four Tauridus's bitter remark, that humanity would have been better served had that time been spent engraving the disintegrating words onto stone.

Gravitronics, cybereconomics and synthephysics were all unknown in the Late Neogene, when the catastrophe occurred. The economic systems of various ethnic groups called nashens were relatively autonomous, and wholly dependent upon the circulation of papyr, as was the flow of supplies to the Syrtic Tiberis colony on Mars.

Papyralysis ruined a great deal more than the economy. That entire period is rightly named the Era of Papyrocracy, for not only did papyr regulate and coordinate all group activities, but it determined, in some obscure way, the fate of individuals (for example, the "identity papyrs"). The functional and ritual roles of papyr in the folklore of that time (the catastrophe took place when Prechaotic Neogene was at its height) have yet to be fully catalogued. While we do know the meaning of some expressions, others remain empty phrases (cheks, dok-ments, ree-seets, etc.). *In that era one could not be born, grow up, obtain an education, work, travel, marry or die except through the aid and mediation of papyr.*

Only in the light of these facts can one appreciate the full extent of the disaster which struck Earth. The quarantine of whole cities and continents, the construction of hermetically sealed shelters—all such measures failed. The science of the day was helpless against the catalyst's subatomic structure, the product of a most unusual anabiotic evolution. For the first time in history society was threatened with total dissolution. To quote an inscription carved upon the wall of a urinal in the Fris-Ko excavations by an anonymous bard of the cataclysm: "And the heavens above the cities grew dark with clouds of blighted papyr and it rained for forty days and forty nights a dirty rain, and thus with wind and streams of mud was the tale of man washed from the face of the earth forever."

It must have been a cruel blow indeed to the pride of Late Neogene man, who saw himself already reaching the stars. The papyralysis nightmare pervaded all walks of life. Panic hit the cities; people, deprived of their identity, lost their reason; the supply of goods broke down; there were incidents of violence; technology, research and development, schools—all crumbled into nonexistence; power plants could not be repaired for lack of blueprints. The lights went out, and the ensuing darkness was illumined only by the glow of bonfires.

And so the Neogene entered into the Chaotic, which was to last over two hundred years. Obviously, the first quarter-century of the Great Collapse left no written records. We

3

can only guess under what conditions government was maintained and anarchy avoided until the establishment, around mid-century, of the Earth Federation.

The more complex a civilization, the more vital to its existence is the maintenance of the flow of information; hence the more vulnerable it becomes to any disturbance in that flow. Now that flow, the lifeblood of the society, had come to a halt. The last storehouse of information lay in the minds of living experts; to record and preserve that information had priority over all else. But this seemingly simple problem proved insoluble. In the Late Neogene, knowledge was so compartmentalized that no one specialist could possibly assimilate the entirety of his field. Reconstruction consequently demanded tedious, long-term collaboration of different groups of experts. Had the task been undertaken at once—so Polygnostor Laa Baar Eight of our Bermand Historical School tells us—Neogene civilization could have been speedily restored. In answer to the distinguished founder of Neogene Chronologistics, we must point out the activity he postulates could indeed have led to the accumulation of veritable mountains of knowledge—but who would there have been to derive benefit from this? Certainly not the hordes of nomads who left their devastated cities; nor their children, who grew up wild and illiterate. No, civilization could have been saved only at the very moment when industry began to fall apart, construction ceased and transportation ground to a halt, when the starving masses of whole continents first cried out for help, including the colony on Mars, deprived of supplies and threatened with extinction. Clearly the experts could not shut themselves up in ivory towers and take the time to develop new techniques of transcription.

Desperate measures were employed. Certain branches of the amusement industry (such as feelms) *mobilized their entire production to record incoming information on the positions of spaceships and satellites, for collisions were multiplying rapidly. Circuit diagrams were printed, from*

4

memory, on fabrics. All available plastic writing materials were distributed among the schools. Physics professors personally had to tend atomic piles. Emergency teams of scientists flitted from one point of the globe to another. But these were merely tiny particles of order, atoms of organization that quickly dissolved in an ocean of spreading chaos. Shaken as it was by endless upheavals, engaged in a constant struggle against the tide of superstition, illiteracy and ignorance, the stagnant culture of the Chaotic should be judged not by what it lost of the heritage of centuries, but by what it was able to salvage, against all odds.

To check the first fury of the Great Collapse necessitated tremendous sacrifices. Earth's first footholds on Mars had been saved, and technology, that backbone of all civilization, was reconstructed. Microphones and tape banks replaced the storage centers of demolished papyr. Unfortunately, cruel losses were sustained in other areas.

Because the supply of new writing materials failed to meet even the most urgent needs, anything that did not directly serve to save the bare framework of society had to be jettisoned. The humanities suffered the worst. Knowledge was disseminated orally, through lectures; the audiences became the educators of the next generation. This was one of those astonishing primitivisms of Chaotic civilization that rescued Earth from total disaster, though losses in the areas of history, historiography, paleology and paleoesthetics were quite irreparable. Only the smallest fragment of a rich literary legacy was preserved. Millions of volumes of chronicles, priceless relics of the Middle and Late Neogene, turned to dust forever.

At the end of the Chaotic we find a most paradoxical situation: there was a relatively high level of technology, including the active initiation of gravitronics and technobiotics, not to mention the success of cisgalactic mass transport; yet the human race knew next to nothing of its own past. All that survives today of the enormous achievements of the Neogene are a few scattered and unrelated remnants, factual accounts altered beyond all recognition and thoroughly garbled through countless retellings in the oral tradition. Even the most important events are of doubtful chronology.

One must concur with Subgnostor Nappro Leis when he says that papyralysis meant historioparalysis. Only in this perspective can we assess the true value of the work of Prognostor Wid-Wiss who, in his single-handed battle against official historiography, discovered the "Notes from the Neogene," a voice speaking to us across the abyss of centuries, a voice belonging to one of the last inhabitants of the lost land of Ammer-Ka. This monument is all the more precious in that there are no others to rival it in importance; it cannot be compared, for example, with the papyrantic finds made by the archeological expedition of Syrtic Paleognostor Bradrah the Mnemonite at the Marglo shale diggings in the Lower Preneogene. Those finds concern religious beliefs prevalent during the Eighth Dynasty of Ammer-Ka; they speak of various Perils—Black, Red, Yellow—evidently cabalistic incantations connected in some way with the mysterious deity Rayss, to whom burnt offerings were apparently made. But this interpretation is still being debated by the Trans-Sindental and Greater Syrtic Schools, as well as by a group of disciples of the famous Bog-Waad.

Most of the Neogene, we fear, will forever remain shrouded in mystery, for even chronotraction methods have failed to provide the most fundamental details of the social life at that age. Any systematic presentation of those few moments of history which we have been able to re-create goes well beyond the limits of this introduction. So we will limit ourselves to a few remarks in the way of background to the "Notes."

The evolution of ancient beliefs underwent a curious bifurcation. In the first period, the Archeocredonic, various religions were founded upon the recognition of a supernatural, nonmaterial principle, causative with respect to everything in existence. The Archeocredonic left behind

*permanent monuments—the pyramids of the Early Neo-
gene, the excavations of the Mesogene (the Gothic cathedrals
of Lafranss).*

*In the second period, the Neocredonic, faith assumed a
different aspect. The metaphysical principle somehow merged
with the materialistic, the earthly. Worship of the deity Kap-
Eh-Taahl (or, in the Cremonic palimpsests, Kapp-Taah)
became one of the dominant cults of the time. This deity
was revered throughout Ammer-Ka and the faith quickly
spread to Australindia and parts of the European Penin-
sula. Any connection, however, between the cult of Kap-
Eh-Taahl and the graven images of the elephant and the
ass found here and there throughout Ammer-Ka does seem
somewhat doubtful. It was forbidden to utter the name
itself, "Kap-Eh-Taahl" (analogous to the Hebrew inter-
diction); in Ammer-Ka the deity was generally called "Almighty Da-Laahr." But there were many other liturgical
names, and special monastic orders devoted themselves
entirely to an appraisal of their changing status (the Mer-
L-Finches, for example). Indeed, the fluctuation in the accepted value of each of the many names (or were they
attributes?) of Kap-Eh-Taahl remains an enigma to this
day. The difficulty in understanding the true nature of that
last of the Prechaotic religions lies in the fact that Kap-Eh-
Taahl was denied any supernatural existence, was therefore
not a spirit, nor was he even considered a being (which
would help explain the totemistic features of that cult, so
unusual in an age of science)—he was, to all extents and
purposes, equated with assets, liquid, fixed, and hidden,
and had no existence beyond that. However, it has been
shown that in times of economic decline, sacrifices of sugar
cane, coffee, and grain were made to placate the angry
god. This contradiction is deepened by the fact that the
cult of Kap-Eh-Taahl did possess some elements of the doctrine of incarnation, according to which, the world owed
its continuing existence to "sacred property." Any violation
of that doctrine met with the most severe punishment.*

As we know, the epoch of global cybereconomics was

preceded, at the close of the Neogene, by the rise of socio-stasy. As the cult of Kap-Eh-Taahl, mired in complex corpo-rational rites and intricate institutional rituals, began in the course of time to lose one territory after another to the followers of secular sociostatic management, there arose a conflict between the lands still ruled by that anti-quated faith and the remaining world.

Up to the very end—that is, to the formation of the Earth Federation—the center of the most fanatic devotion to Kap-Eh-Taahl was Ammer-Ka, a land governed by a series of dynasties of Prez-tendz. These were not high priests of Kap-Eh-Taahl in the strict sense of the word. It was during the Nineteenth Dynasty that the Prez-tendz (or Prexy-dents, in the nomenclature of the Thyrric School) built the Pentagon. What was it, that first of many granite leviathans, that stern edifice which ushered in the twilight of the Neogene? Prehistorians of the Aquillian School con-sidered the Pentagon's tombs for Prez-tendz, analogous to the Egyptian pyramids. This hypothesis was discarded in the light of subsequent discoveries, as was the theory that these were shrines to Kap-Eh-Taahl, where crusades were planned against the Heathen Dog, or strategies devised to ensure his successful conversion.

Lacking the firsthand information needed to solve this puzzle, undoubtedly the key to an understanding of the whole final phase (the Twenty-fourth and Twenty-fifth Dynasties), our historians turned to the Temporal Institute for help. The Institute's full cooperation made possible the application of the latest technological developments in chronotraction to the task of penetrating the riddle of the Pentagons. We sent 290 probes into the far past, tapping 17 trillion erg-seconds from the time wells that orbit the Moon.

According to the theory of chronotraction, movement back in time is practicable only at a considerable distance from objects of great mass, since their proximity consumes staggering amounts of energy. Consequently, sightings of the past had to be taken from probes placed high in the stratosphere. Their sudden appearance and disappearance in the sky must have mystified the people of the Neogene. Prodoctor Two Sturlprans maintains that the projection of a retrochronal probe would show up in the past as a bulging disc, not unlike two horizontal saucers floating rim-to-rim through space.

Chronotraction yielded an abundance of data, including authentic photoshots of the First Pentagon soon after its construction. This building, indeed a pentagon, each side measuring 460 feens, was a veritable labyrinth of steel and concrete. Histognostor Ser Een estimates the corridors ran about seventeen to eighteen of their mylz. The entrances were guarded day and night by over two hundred priests of lower rank. Further time delving, prompted by the chronicles excavated in the ruins of Waa-Sheetn, led to the discovery of the Second Pentagon, a much less imposing structure than the First, as most of it lay beneath the ground. Certain passages from the chronicles pointed to the existence of yet another, a Third Pentagon. This was to have been a closed, completely independent unit, a state within a state, by virtue of sophisticated camouflaging and enormous reserves of food, water and compressed air. However, after systematic chronoaxial soundings were taken over the entire length and breadth of twentieth-century Ammer-Ka and revealed not a trace of any such structure, most historians accepted the thesis that the Waa-Sheetn chronicles spoke of the Third Pentagon in a figurative sense only, that the building was raised purely in the minds and hearts of the faithful, and that the propagation of the legend was designed to uplift the flagging spirits of those few remaining followers of Kap-Eh-Taahl.

So stood the official version of our historiography when the young Prognostor Wid-Wiss began his archeological career.

Wid-Wiss reexamined all the available materials and published a treatise in which he maintained that, as the power of the Prez-tendz began to wane and their dominions diminish, they resolved to build a new seat of government, one far from all populated areas, somewhere in the mountainous regions of Ammer-Ka and hidden deep beneath the rocks, that this last refuge of Kap-Eh-Taahl might be inaccessible to the uninitiated. Wid-Wiss held that the postulated Pentagon of the Last Dynasty was a kind of collective military brain whose task was twofold: first, to watch over and preserve the purity of the faith, and secondly, to convert those peoples of the world who had abandoned the true path.

But Wid-Wiss's treatise was pooh-poohed by the experts; it clearly ran counter to most of the known facts. Critics like Supergnostors Yoo Na Vaak, Quirlsto and Pisuovo of the Martian School of Comparative Paleography pointed out the many contradictions in Wid-Wiss's chronology.

For example, the Last Pentagon had been built, according to Wid-Wiss, only a few decades before the papyr catastrophe. But if this Third Pentagon had really existed, argued the critics, the Prez-tendz within would have surely taken advantage of the postpapyr anarchy and attempted to conquer the world in the very first days of the Chaotic. And even had such an attempt to overthrow the Federation been thwarted, some trace of it would have survived in the oral tradition. Yet our historiography notes nothing of the kind.

Wid-Wiss defended his hypothesis, claiming that when the populace of Ammer-Ka went over to the side of the "heretics" and joined the Federation, the priests of the Last Pentagon ordered it to be completely sealed off from the outside world. So the underground Moloch isolated itself from the rest of humanity and endured to the Chaotic without the least knowledge of what was taking place on the surface of the earth.

This absolute, hermetic isolation of a community of priests and warriors of Kap-Eh-Taahl did seem, Wid-Wiss admitted, a bit unlikely. So he went on to speculate that the Last Pentagon may have possessed scanning devices on the outside. He did not think, however, that the collective military brain of the Last Dynasty was capable of any offensive or even diversive action. It certainly could not have attacked or engineered a coup against the Federation, for once the colossus had buried itself in rock and severed all ties with the future course of history, it was imprisoned not only by impenetrable walls but by the very nature of its internal organization. From that time on it thrived exclusively on the myth, the legend of the glory that was Kap-Eh-Taahl, and investigated, rooted out and waged bitter war against heresy—the heresy within.

Our Histognostors answered these arguments with a stony silence. But Wid-Wiss did not give in. For twenty-seven years, with only a handful of loyal colleagues to help him, he combed the Rocket Mountains from end to end. Just when almost everyone had forgotten him, his stubbornness was dramatically vindicated. On 28 Mey 3146, the head archeological team, having cleared away several hundred tons of rubble at the foot of Haar-Vurd Peak, stood before a convex shield, cleverly camouflaged, excellently preserved: this was the entrance to the Last Pentagon.

Exploration of the underground building, however, proved extremely difficult and demanded extraordinary methods. In the seventy-second year of its retreat from the world, the Pentagon of the Last Dynasty succumbed to a natural disaster. A slight shift in the mountain's granite core produced a fissure that traveled down through several strata until it came into contact with magma. The building's concrete protective shell could not withstand the volcanic pressure; molten lava entered and filled the interior from top to bottom. And so that strange anthill of the last of the Prez-tendz became a giant fossil and, as such, waited one thousand six hundred and eighty years to be discovered.

It is not our task to describe here the tremendous archeological wealth of the Third Pentagon diggings. We refer the interested reader to the many volumes devoted specially to that subject. Only a few remarks remain to be added to this introduction to the "Notes."

The "Notes" were discovered in the third year of excavation, on the fourth level, within an intricate corridor system where there were several sanitation facilities. In one of these facilities, filled as the rest with igneous rock, were two human skeletons and, beneath them, a scroll of papyr—the "Notes."

The reader will see for himself that the daring suppositions of Histognostor Wid-Wiss were for the most part quite accurate. The "Notes" portray the fate of a community locked beneath the earth, a community that refused to allow the infiltration of any news of real events, pretending it constituted the Brain, the Headquarters of an empire that extended even to the most remote galaxies. In time the pretense became belief, the belief a certainty. The reader will witness how the fanatical servants of Kap-Eh-Taahl created the myth of the Antibuilding, how they spent their lives in mutual surveillance, in tests of loyalty and devotion to the Mission, even when the last figment of that Mission's reality had become an impossibility and nothing remained but to sink ever deeper into the pit of collective madness.

Our historiography has not yet passed final judgment on the "Notes," commonly called, for the location of their discovery, "Memoirs Found in a Bathtub." Then too, no agreement has been reached as to when and in what order certain parts of the manuscript were written. The Hyberiad Gnostors, for example, consider the first twelve pages apocryphal, an addition of later years. But the reader will hardly be interested in such technical matters. Let us then be silent and allow this last message from the Neogene, the Era of Papyrocracy, to speak to us in its own voice.

1

. . . I couldn't seem to find the right room—none of them had the number designated on my pass. First I wound up at the Department of Verification, then the Department of Misinformation, then some clerk from the Pressure Section advised me to try level eight, but on level eight they ignored me, and later I got stuck in a crowd of military personnel—the corridors rang with their vigorous marching back and forth, the slamming of doors, the clicking of heels, and over that martial noise I could hear the distant music of bells, the tinkling of medals. Now and then janitors would go by with steaming percolators, now and then I would stumble into rest rooms where secretaries hastily renewed their make-up, now and then agents disguised as elevator men would strike up conversations—one of them had an artificial leg and he took me from floor to floor so many times that after a while he began waving to me from a distance and even stopped photographing me with the camera-carnation in his lapel. By noon we were buddies, and he showed me his pride and joy, a tape recorder under the elevator floor. But I was getting more and more depressed and couldn't share his enthusiasm.

Stubborn, I went from room to room and pestered people with questions, though the answers were invariably wrong. I was still on the outside, still excluded from that ceaseless flow of secrecy that kept the Building strong. But I had to get in somewhere, find an entry at some point, no matter what. Twice I ended up in a storage cellar and leafed through some secret documents lying about. But there was nothing there of any value to me. After several hours of this, thoroughly annoyed and hungry as well (it was past lunchtime and there wasn't even a cafeteria to be found), I decided to take a different tack.

I recalled that the highest concentration of tall, gray officers was on the fourth level, so I headed there, opened a door bearing the sign BY APPOINTMENT ONLY and entered an empty reception room, from there went through a side door marked KNOCK BEFORE ENTERING and into a conference room full of moldering mobilization plans. Here I ran into a problem—there were two doors. One said NO ADMITTANCE, the other CLOSED. After some deliberation I decided on the second door—the correct choice as it turned out, since this was the office of General Kashenblade himself, the Commander in Chief. I walked in, and the officer who was on duty at the time led me to the Chief without asking any questions.

A powerful, bald old man, Kashenblade stirred his coffee. His head was perched upon the collar of his uniform; the bristling, many-folded jowls covered the galactic insignia and stripes like a bib. The desk was cluttered with phones and surrounded by computer consoles, speakers, buttons, and in the center was a row of labeled glass jars—specimens, apparently, though I couldn't see a thing in them apart from the alcohol. Kashenblade, the veins bulging on his shiny pate, was busy pushing buttons to silence the phones as soon as they began to ring. When several rang together, he rammed his fist into the whole bank of buttons. Then he noticed me. In the silence that followed there was only the grim tapping of his teaspoon.

"So there you are!" he snapped. It was a powerful voice.

"Yes," I answered.

"Wait, don't tell me, I have a good memory," he growled, watching me from under those bushy eyebrows. "X-27 contrastellar to Cygnus Eps, right?"

"No," I said.

"No? No! Well then. Morbilantrix B-KuK 81 dash Operation Nail? B as in Bipropodal?"

"No," I said, trying to maneuver my pass before his eyes. He waved it aside impatiently.

"No?" He looked hurt. Then he looked pensive. He

stirred his coffee. The phone rang—his hand came down on the button like a lion's paw.

"Plastic?" he shot at me.

"Plastic?" I said. "Well, hardly... I'm just an ordinary—"

Kashenblade stilled the rising din of phones with one quick slap and looked me over once more.

"Operation Cyclogastrosaur... Ento-mo... pentacla," he kept trying, unwilling to admit to any gap in his infallibility. When I failed to respond, he suddenly leaned forward and roared:

"Out!!"

And it really looked as if he himself were ready to throw me out bodily. But I was too determined—also too much a civilian—to obey that order. I held my ground and kept the pass under his nose. At last Kashenblade reluctantly took it and—without even examining it—tossed it into a drawer of some machine, which immediately began to hum and whisper. Kashenblade listened to the machine; his face clouded over and his eyes glittered. He gave me a furtive glance and started pressing buttons. The phones rang out together like a brass band. He silenced them and pressed other buttons: now the speakers drowned one another out with numbers and cryptonyms. He stood there and listened with a scowl, his eyelid twitching. But I could see the storm had passed.

"All right, hand over your scrap of paper!" he barked.

"I already did ..."

"To whom?"

"To you."

"To me?"

"To you, sir."

"When? Where?"

"Just a moment ago, and you threw—" I began, then bit my tongue.

Kashenblade glared at me and opened the drawer of that machine: it was empty, my pass had disappeared. Not that I believed for a moment that this was an accident; in fact, I had suspected for some time now that the Cosmic Command, obviously no longer able to supervise every assignment on an individual basis when there were literally trillions of matters in its charge, had switched over to a random system. The assumption would be that every document, circulating endlessly from desk to desk, must eventually hit upon the right one. A time-consuming procedure, perhaps, but one that would never fail. The Universe itself operated on the same principle. And for an institution as everlasting as the Universe—certainly our Building was such an institution—the speed at which these meanderings and perturbations took place was of no consequence.

At any rate, my pass was gone. Kashenblade slammed the drawer shut and observed me for a while, blinking. I stood there, my hands at my side, uncomfortably aware of their emptiness. His blinking became more insistent as I stood there, then positively fierce. I blinked back. That seemed to pacify him.

"Okay," he muttered, pushing a few buttons. Computers churned, multicolored tapes snaked out onto the desk. He tore them off bit by bit, read them, absentmindedly set other machines going, machines that made copies and destroyed originals. Finally a white folder emerged with INSTRUCTIONS B-66-PAPRA-LABL in letters so large I could read them from across the desk.

"Your assignment . . . a Mission, a Special Mission," General Kashenblade said with tremendous gravity. "Deep penetration, subversion—were you ever there?" he asked with a blink.

"Where?"

"There."

He lifted his head; once again the eyelids fluttered. I didn't know what to answer.

"And *this* is an agent," he said with disgust. "An agent . . . a modern agent . . ." He grew morose. The word "agent" was stretched out of shape and became a taunt, it whistled through his teeth, every consonant and vowel was chewed and slowly tortured. Then he exploded: "Everything has to be spelled out, eh? Don't you read the papers? Stars, for example —tell me about the stars! What do they do? Well?!"

"They shine," I said doubtfully.

"They shine, he says! All right, how? How do they shine? Tell me how!"

And he pointed to his eyelids.

"Uh, they twinkle—they blink—they—wink," I answered in an involuntary whisper.

"How clever he is! At last! They wink! Yes, they wink! But *when* do they wink? Do you know when? I bet you don't! And that's the kind of material I have to work with around here! At *night!* They wink, they cower under cover of night!!"

He roared like a lion. I stood at attention, straight as an arrow, waiting for the storm to pass. But it was not passing. Kashenblade, puffed up and purple to the top of his bald head, shook the room with his bellow, shook the Building itself.

"And the spiral nebulae?! Well?! Don't tell me you don't know what *that* means! SPY-ral!! And the expanding universe, the retreating galaxies! Where are they going? What are they running from? And the Doppler shift to the *red!!* Highly suspicious—no, more! A clear admission of guilt!!"

He gave me a withering look, sat back and said in a voice cold with contempt:

"Moron!"

"Now just a minute—" I flared up.

"What? What was that?! Just a minute—? Ah yes, the password! Good, good. Just a minute . . . the password, yes, that's better . . ."

And he attacked the buttons—the machines rattled like rain on a tin roof, green and gold ribbons spun out and coiled on the desk. The old man read them avidly.

"Good!" he concluded, clutching them in his fists. "Your Mission. Conduct an on-the-spot investigation. Verify. Search. Destroy. Incite. Inform. Over and out. On the nth day nth hour sector n subsector n rendezvous with N. Stop. Salary group under cryptonym Bareback. Voucher for unlimited oxygen. Payment by weight for denunciations, and sporadic. Report regularly. Your contact is Pyra-LiP, your cover Lyra-PiP. When you fall in action, posthumous decoration with the Order of the Top Secret, full honors, salutes, memorial plaque, and a written recommendation in your dossier. Any questions?"

"But if I don't fall in action?" I asked.

An indulgent smile spread across the general's face.

"A wise guy," he said. "I had to get a wise guy. Very funny. Okay, so much for the jokes. You have your Mission now. Do you know, do you understand what *that* is?" His lofty brow unwrinkled, the golden medals on his chest gleamed. "A Mission—it's a wonderful thing! And Special —a *Special* Mission! Words fail me! Go, go my boy, God be with you, and keep on your toes!"

"I'll do my best," I said. "But what exactly is the assignment?"

He pressed several buttons, phones rang, he silenced them. The purple pate slowly turned pink. He eyed me benevolently, like a father.

"Oh," he said, "extremely hazardous. But remember, it is not for me! *I* am not sending you! The Country! The Common Good! Yes, yes . . . you, I know . . . it'll be hard, no picnic, a tough nut to crack . . . You'll see! Tough, but it must be done, because . . . because . . ."

"Our Duty," I prompted.

He beamed. He rose. The medals on his chest swayed and jingled like bells, a hush fell over the machines, the phones grew silent and the lights dimmed. He approached me, he gave me his powerful, hairy hand, the hand of an old soldier. His eyes bored right through me, the bushy brows knitted in a solemn squint. Thus we stood, united by a handshake, the Commander in Chief and the secret agent.

"Our Duty!" were his words. "Well said, my boy! Our Duty! Take care!"

I saluted, about-faced, exited, hearing on the way out how he sipped his cold coffee. Kashenblade—now there was a man.

2

Still a little dazed by my conversation with the Chief, I entered the main office. The secretaries were all busy putting on lipstick and stirring coffee. A wad of papers tumbled out of the mail chute: my orders, signed by General Kashenblade. One clerk stamped them "classified" and handed them to another, who put them on index cards, which in turn were filed away, retrieved, coded by machine—then the key was destroyed, all the original papers burned, the ashes sifted, registered and sealed in an envelope bearing my number, and the envelope was dispatched by pneumatic tube to an unknown vault. But I was unable to pay proper attention to this procedure; the unexpected turn of events had left me quite numb. General Kashenblade's cryptic remarks clearly indicated matters so secret that one could only hint at them. Though sooner or later I would have to be apprised of their substance. How else could I accomplish my Mission? Did the Mission have anything to do with my original pass? But that question was utterly insignificant in the light of this new, all-too-sudden career of mine.

My musings were interrupted by the arrival of a young officer who introduced himself as the Chief's undercover aide, Lieutenant Blanderdash. This Lieutenant Blanderdash shook my hand, told me he had been assigned to my person, led me to an office across the hall, offered me some coffee, began to extol my extraordinary abilities (they had to be extraordinary indeed for Kashenblade to have given me such a tough nut to crack), and also marveled at the naturalness of my face, particularly the nose—then I realized he assumed it was false. I stirred my coffee in silence, deciding that reticence was the best policy. After some fifteen minutes he took me through an officers' passageway to a service elevator. We broke the seal and rode it down.

"Incidentally," he said as soon as we stepped out, "do you yawn much?"

"Not that I know of. Why?"

"Oh, nothing. When a person yawns, one can look inside, you know. You don't snore, by any chance?"

"No."

"Wonderful. You can't imagine how many of our people have come to a bad end by snoring."

"What happened to them?" I was reckless enough to ask.

But he only smiled and fingered his insignia. "Perhaps you would like to see the displays? They're right on this level—over there by the columns. Our Department of Collections."

"Sure," I replied, "but do we have the time?"

"No problem," he said, steering me in the right direction. "Anyway, this is not to satisfy an idle curiosity. In our profession the more one knows, the better."

Blanderdash opened an ordinary white door, behind which was solid steel. He worked a combination lock and the steel slid away, revealing an enormous, windowless but brightly lit hall. The coffered ceiling was supported by pillars; the walls were covered with tapestries and hangings in black, gold and silver. I had never seen anything so magnificent before. Between the columns across the highly polished parquet stood the showcases, cabinets, vitrines on slender metal legs, chests with their lids open. The one nearest me was filled with small items that gleamed like jewels. They were cuff links, and there must have been a million of them. From another chest rose a mound of pearls. Blanderdash led me to the glass cases: on velvet cushions lay artificial ears, noses, bridges, fingernails, warts, eyelashes, boils and humps, some displayed in cross section to show the gears and springs inside. As I stepped back, I stumbled against the chest of pearls and shuddered: they were teeth—snaggleteeth and tiny teeth, buck teeth, teeth with cavities and teeth without, milk teeth, eye teeth, wisdom teeth . . .

My guide smiled and pointed to the nearest tapestry. I

21

took a closer look: beards, goatees, sideburns, mutton-chops, all sewn onto a nylon base in such a fashion that the blond ones represented, against a brunette background, the national seal. In the next room, even more spacious than the first, were more glass cases. These contained artifacts and keepsakes such as cheeses or decks of cards. From the pine ceiling-beams hung artificial limbs, corsets, clothing. There were artificial insects too, crafted with a precision that only a great and wealthy power could have summoned the means to achieve. The insect display alone filled several shelves. Blanderdash did not intrude with explanations, certain that the corpora delicti assembled here would speak for themselves. But now and then, whenever he thought I might overlook some particularly interesting item in the abundance of things to see, he pointed it out discreetly. For example, he directed my attention to a great quantity of poppy seed placed on white silk under a strong magnifying lens. This enabled me to notice that each individual seed had been painstakingly hollowed out. Amazed, I turned to ask him what this meant. But he cut me off with a commiserating smile and a shrug, and to make his meaning clear, silently mouthed the word "classified." Only when we left did he casually remark, "Interesting trophies, aren't they?"

The next room was even more magnificent. I looked up and saw an enormous tapestry on the opposite wall, a true masterpiece in auburn and black depicting the birth of a nation. After some hesitation, Blanderdash pointed out one dignitary's coat in the panorama: the lapels were neatly trimmed black sideburns; I was given to understand they originally belonged to an enemy agent this dignitary had unmasked.

A cold draft from behind the columns suggested a whole suite of rooms beyond. I no longer looked at the exhibits but followed my guide meekly, quite lost in all this splendor, dazzled by the glitter and the spotlights. We went past sections on the opening of safes, the tempting of agents, the drilling through of walls and mountains, the drying up of seas; I gaped at many-storied machines, machines to copy mobilization plans at any distance, machines to change night into artificial day and vice versa. We crossed a large hall under an immense crystal dome used to simulate sunspots and falsify planetary orbits; replicas of fake constellations and imitation galaxies gleamed on plaques of precious stone. Behind the walls powerful vacuum pumps worked to maintain the low density of air and high level of radiation required to keep the counterfeit atoms and electrons functioning smoothly. My head was spinning—there was too much to take in. Blanderdash noticed my condition and asked me to follow him to the exit.

Earlier, halfway through the Department of Collections, I had prepared some compliments to deliver after seeing the entire exhibit. But now I couldn't utter a single word. Blanderdash understood my silence and said nothing. At the elevator two officers approached us, saluted, begged my pardon, and took Blanderdash aside. Blanderdash seemed surprised—he said something, eyebrows raised, but they answered with negative gestures and pointed in my direction. With this, the brief exchange ended. Blanderdash left with the older officer, and the younger approached and explained with an ingratiating smile that he was to accompany me to Department N.

I saw no reason to protest. But as we stepped back into the elevator, I began to question him about my former guide.

"Did you say something?" the officer asked, lowering his ear to my mouth and at the same time pressing his hand to his chest, as if in pain.

"Yes, about Blanderdash. Was he called away on duty? I know I shouldn't ask—"

"Not at all, not at all," the officer said hastily. A slow, peculiar smile widened his thin lips. "Could you say that again?" he asked, suddenly pensive.

"Say what?"

"The name."

"Blanderdash? But . . . that is his name, isn't it?"

"Oh, I'm sure it is, I'm sure it is." But his smile grew more pensive.

"Blanderdash," he muttered as the elevator came to a stop. "Blanderdash . . . of course . . ."

I wondered what the "of course" was supposed to mean, whether or not it was for my benefit—but just then the elevator opened and we were walking quickly down a corridor toward one of those white doors. He ushered me into a long, narrow room without windows and snapped the door shut behind me. There were four desks under low lamps and an officer at each, laboring over stacks of paper and in shirtsleeves because of the heat. One of them sat up and fixed his dark eyes on me.

"State your business."

I subdued my impatience.

"Special Mission by order of General Kashenblade."

If I thought the other officers would look up at these words, I was greatly mistaken.

"Your name?" I was asked in the same brisk manner. This officer had the muscular hands of an athlete, tanned, with a small tattoo in code.

I gave my name. He pressed the keys of a machine on his desk.

"The nature of the Mission?"

"I'm to be briefed on that here."

"Oh?" he said. He took his jacket off the chair, put it on, buttoned it, adjusted the epaulets and headed for a side door.

"Follow me."

I followed him, looking around and realizing for the first time that the officer who had brought me here never entered, but remained in the hall.

My new guide turned a desk lamp on and introduced himself: "Seconddecoder Dasherblar. Have a seat."

He pressed a buzzer. A young secretary brought two cups

of coffee. Dasherblar sat opposite me and sipped his coffee without a word.

"You're to be briefed on the goal of your Mission?" he said at last.

"Yes."

"H'm. Your Mission. It's difficult, complicated . . . unusual too—I'm sorry, your name?"

"Still the same," I replied with a faint smile.

The officer smiled in return. He had beautiful teeth; his whole face radiated sincerity and openness in that moment.

"Cigarette?"

"No thanks, I don't smoke."

"Good, very good. It's a bad habit, a very bad habit . . . Well, then . . . Excuse me a moment."

He got up, switched on the overhead lights, went to a huge metal safe and turned seven combination dials in succession. The massive steel plate slid noiselessly aside, and he began to look through a file of folders within.

"Now, your instructions," he said. But just then a buzzer sounded. He turned and looked at me. "Must be important. Could you wait? It'll only take a minute."

Dasherblar went out, shutting the door quietly, leaving me alone with the open safe.

Was this a test? How could they be so obvious about it, so transparent? I was annoyed. For a while I didn't budge; then I happened to turn my head toward the safe. Immediately I looked away—but there was a mirror, and it showed all the contents of the safe, all the secret documents. I thought of counting the wooden panels in the parquet floor. But the floor here was linoleum. I inspected my knuckles. I was getting angry. Why shouldn't I look where I pleased? So I looked: the folders were black, green, pink, a few were yellow and had saucer-like seals hanging from strings. One folder in particular, the one on top, was dog-eared. That was probably it. Anyway, the Chief of Staff himself gave me the Mission, if there was any trouble I could always mention his name—but wait, what was I thinking of?!

I looked at my watch: ten minutes had passed. Complete silence. My chair became more uncomfortable with each passing minute. I crossed my legs—that was worse. I got up, straightened the crease in my trousers, sat down again. Even the desk on which I rested my elbow irritated me. I stretched. That took a minute. My stomach began to growl. I drank the rest of my coffee and contemplated the sugar at the bottom of the cup. I no longer dared even look at the open safe. Another glance at my watch: an hour had gone by.

By the second hour I gave up all hope that the officer would return. Something must have happened. But what? Was he suddenly recalled, like Blanderdash? Or was it Dasherbland? No, Dashenblar. Dashenblade? For the life of me I couldn't remember—my stomach growled too much. I got up and paced the floor. Almost three hours now, alone with an open safe full of secret documents—heads would roll, including my own! Oh, he fixed me, all right, that . . . whatever his name was! Suppose someone asked me who I was waiting for? I decided to leave. But which way? The way I came in? They would question me, and my story wouldn't hold up—I could feel that. The judges would smile. "You mean to tell us that an officer whose name you can't even remember left you alone with an open safe? Come now, let's think up something a little more original!" It was hot, sweat streamed down my neck and back. My throat was dry. I tried to close the safe. The bolts wouldn't lock. No matter how much I turned the dials, the door stubbornly sprang back. It refused to stay shut. Then there were footsteps in the hall. I jumped back, caught my sleeve on the file and the whole stack of folders tumbled out onto the floor. The doorknob moved—I lost my head—I crawled under the desk. All I could see of the man who entered were black, pointed shoes. For a moment he stood still. Then he quietly closed the door and tiptoed over to the safe, out of my field of vision. I heard the rustle of paper and then another sound, a faint clicking, like a distant bell. Of course! He was photographing the secret documents! That meant this wasn't the other officer, but . . .

I crept out from under the desk and crawled towards the door. Then, as I reached it, I sprang up and leaped out into the hall. In the split second it took me to slam the door, I caught a glimpse of a pale, horrified face and a camera falling from trembling hands—then I was far away. I walked straight ahead, keeping an even step, passed various bends and curves in the hall, rows of white doors through which I could hear the muffled noise of office work and a faint bell-like tinkling, a sound that was no longer a mystery to me.

Now what? Report the whole incident? But obviously, that man would no longer be there. All that would remain was an open safe, papers strewn about the room. Suddenly I froze—I had left my name in the office there. They knew me, they were searching for me. The whole Building must have been alerted by now; all staircases, exits, elevators were being watched . . .

I looked around. The corridors were filled with the usual activity. Several officers were carrying folders, folders as like the ones in the safe as peas in a pod. A janitor went by with a steaming percolator. An elevator opened right in front of me and two adjutants stepped out. They didn't even see me. Why wasn't anything happening? Why wasn't I being hunted down? Could it be that . . . that all this . . . was only a test?

I made a quick decision. The nearest door read: 76/941. No, I didn't like it, I moved on . . . 76/950 suited me. Knock? What for?

As I entered, two secretaries were stirring their coffee, and a third arranged sandwiches on a plate. They ignored me. I passed them and tried another door, the next room. I walked in.

"So you finally got here! Come in, come in, make yourself comfortable."

A tiny old man in gold spectacles smiled at me from behind the desk. His hair was white as milk, and so sparse that pink skin innocently peeked out here and there. The eyes were like small nuts, the smile was cordial, the gestures full of welcome. I sank into a soft armchair.

"General Kashenblade—" I began. But he didn't let me finish.

"Of course, of course . . . will you allow me?"

His palsied fingers pressed a few buttons. Then he rose with great ceremony, a grave smile on his face. The lower lid of his left eye had a slight twitch.

"Undereavesdropper Blassenkash. Permit me to shake your hand."

"You know me?" I asked.

"And how could I not know you?"

"Oh—really?" I stammered, completely thrown off balance. "Then—then perhaps you have my instructions?"

"Why certainly! But there is no hurry, no hurry . . . So many years of isolation . . . the zodiac . . . how the thought saddens my heart! At such great distances, you know . . . a man finds it hard to believe, to reconcile himself to the fact, don't you think? I'm an old man, I talk too much . . . You know, I never flew, not once . . . Well, that's our work . . . always behind a desk . . . sleevelets, you know, to protect the cuffs—I wore out eighteen pair." He shook his head. "So you see, that's how it is . . . an old man rambles on . . ."

He conducted me to an enormous room, all in green and large enough to be a banquet hall. The floor glistened like a lake; on the far side stood a green table and chairs. Our footsteps echoed as if we were in a cathedral. The old man tottered along at my side, smiling, adjusting the spectacles that kept slipping down his nose. At the table he pulled out a chair for me, beautifully upholstered and with an elegant crest on the back. He sat in another, stirred his coffee with a withered hand, took a sip and whispered, "Cold." I waited. He leaned over confidentially.

"Surprised?"

"I—well, not really, no."

"Eh, you can tell me, I'm an old man. But I don't insist . . . I don't insist . . . That would be, on my part, of course —but then you see, the utter loneliness, and the gates of mystery opening, inviting, the dark abyss . . . temptation— ah, it's only human! Understandable! And what is curiosity? The first reflex of a newborn baby, the most natural of impulses, the primal wish to find the Cause, the Cause of the Effect, the Effect that in turn causes Action, and so a continuity is established . . . the chains that bind us . . . and it all began so innocently!"

"Excuse me," I asked, confused, "what are you getting at?"

"Just this!" he shouted in a thin, piping voice. "Just this!" He leaned closer, the gold frames of his spectacles gleaming. "Here we have the Cause—there the Effect! What am I getting at, you ask? The mind cannot leave such questions unanswered, it fills in the gaps, takes a little here, adds a little there . . ."

"Look," I said, "I really don't understand what all this—"

"In a minute, in a minute, young man! Not all is darkness! I shall explain the best I can . . . Forgive a poor old man who does his best . . . What did you want to know?"

"My instructions."

"Your—*what?*" He was clearly surprised.

I said nothing. He closed his eyes, his wrinkled lips moved as if he were counting: ". . . sixteen, take away one, carry the six . . ."

He grinned.

"Perfect, perfect. Your instructions, your papers, your documents, your blueprints . . . war plans, strategic calcu- lations, everything secret, top secret . . . Oh, what the en- emy wouldn't give! Despicable, conniving, wanting to take over! If only for one night—one hour!" The old man almost sang the words. "And so he sends out his agents, well- briefed, well-schooled, well-disguised, and they sneak in, destroy, steal, copy—and their name is Legion!" he cried in a quavering voice, clutching his spectacles with both hands. "And what can we do? . . . In a hundred, in a thousand cases we unmask the conspiracy, cut off the evil hand, extract the deadly poison . . . But the attempts are renewed, two arms grow where one was severed . . . and the end result is the same, inevitable. What one can hide, another can find. The natural course of events, young man . . ."

He ran out of breath and gave a piteous smile. I waited.

"But just imagine, what if there were more than one plan? Not two, not four—a thousand! Ten thousand! A million! Could they steal that? Yes, they could, but then the first plan would contradict the seventh, the seventh would contradict the nine hundred and eighty-first, and the nine hundred and eighty-first would contradict all the others. Each one says something else, no two are alike—which is the right one, the real one, the one and only one?"

"Clever!" I said.

"Yes!!" His cry of triumph ended in a fit of coughing, a fit so violent that his spectacles flew off. He caught them in midair. I could have sworn a piece of the nose had also come off—no, it must have been my imagination. The poor old man was blue in the face, his wrinkled lips trembled.

"Now . . . now imagine thousands of safes, thousands of original documents . . . everywhere, everywhere, on every level of the Building, all under lock and key, each one an original, each one entirely unique—millions and millions of them, and each one different!"

"Wait a minute!" I said. "Are you trying to tell me that—instead of only one operational plan, there are—"

"Exactly! Your grasp of the situation is perfect, young man!"

"But there must be at least one correct plan. I mean, if we ever had to . . . if the necessity arose . . ."

I didn't finish, struck by the change that had come over him. He was looking at me as if I had suddenly turned into a monster.

"Oh . . . is that what you think?" he rasped, his eyelids fluttering like dried-up butterflies.

"Well, not really," I replied cautiously. "Let's suppose that everything is as you say. How does it all affect me? And—if I may ask—what connection does it have with the Mission?"

"Mission?"

His smile, humble and hesitant, was altogether too sweet.

"The Special Mission assigned to me by—but I told you that at the very beginning, didn't I? Our Commander in Chief, General Kashenblade."

"Kashenblade?"

"Surely you know the name of your own Chief!"

"Excuse me," he whispered after a long silence, "would you mind if I . . . if I leave you for a moment? I won't be long . . ."

"I'm sorry," I said, politely but firmly holding his arm when he attempted to get up. "You are not going anywhere until we settle this. I came for instructions, I am waiting to receive them."

The old man trembled.

"But . . . but, my dear man . . . how am I to understand this? . . ."

"Cause and Effect," I said crisply. "My assignment, if you please!"

He paled, but was silent.

"I am waiting."

No answer.

"Why did you tell me about the millions of plans? Or perhaps I should ask *who* told you to tell me? You don't feel like talking? Very well. I have time, I can wait."

He only clasped his palsied hands and lowered his head.

"What are you doing?" I shouted and grabbed his arm. The face twisted in a hideous grimace and the eyes bulged in terror; he was sucking the ring on his finger. There was a faint click, metal on metal, and I felt the rigid muscles turn to water. A second later I was holding a corpse. I let it fall to the floor. The spectacles came off and with them a fold of silver hair and baby pink skin, revealing a shock of jet-black hair underneath. I stood there, the dead man at my feet, and listened to the pounding of my heart. I looked around frantically—I had to escape, any moment now someone could come in and find me with the body of a man who had held some important post. Underdecoder? Eavesdropper? It didn't matter now. I made for the door, but stopped halfway. I couldn't possibly get through, they would recognize me for sure. And then how would I explain? An alibi . . .

I went back and lifted the body; the wig slid off—how much younger he looked in death! Carefully, I put the wig back on, fought down a wave of revulsion, gripped the body under the arms and dragged it to the door. I could say he had a fainting spell—that would have to do.

The office was empty. There were two doors: one led to the secretaries, the other probably led to the hall. I sat him in his chair behind the desk. He slumped. I tried to make him sit up. Impossible—the left arm dangled over the chair. I left the body as it was and ran out the second door. I didn't care what happened now!

3

It looked like the lunch hour—officers, clerks, secretaries, everyone flocked to the elevators. I fell in with the largest group and was soon riding down—away from the scene of the crime, the farther the better!

Lunch wasn't very good: a limp salad, leathery roast beef, the usual mashed potatoes, vile coffee as black as tar. No one paid. Fortunately there was no conversation, not even about the food; they were all busy solving puzzles instead—crosswords and word ladders, anagrams and cryptograms, brain teasers and riddles. To avoid calling attention to myself, I scribbled something on a scrap of paper I found in my pocket. After an hour of this, I elbowed my way back to the hall. Now people were returning to work, taking the elevators up. The crowd was thinning fast, I had to find someplace to go, so I jumped on one of the last elevators and got out at the first stop. The hall here, like all the others I had seen so far, had no windows. Rows of gleaming white doors stretched out on either side, with milky globes over the door signs: 76/947, 76/948, 76/950 . . .

I stopped. That number, that same number! How did I, wandering aimlessly, happen to return exactly to this spot? Behind that door—if they hadn't discovered it yet—was a body propped up at a desk, a pair of twisted gold spectacles perched on its nose . . .

Someone was coming. It took considerable effort not to break into a run. A tall officer without a cap came around the corner. I stepped aside to let him pass, but he walked up to me with a vague smile.

"Step this way, please," he said in a lowered voice, indicating the door next to the one with the body.

"I don't understand," I said, also lowering my voice. "There must be some mistake."

"Oh no, there's no mistake. In here, please."

He opened the door and I found myself in a bright yellow office. Other than a desk and a few telephones and chairs, there was no office equipment. I stayed near the door. The officer closed it quietly and walked around me.

"Won't you have a seat?"

"You know who I am?" I asked slowly.

"Of course." He nodded, bringing me a chair.

"What is there to talk about?"

"I understand you perfectly. Let me assure you that I'll do all in my power to keep this strictly confidential."

"Confidential? What do you mean?"

He came so close that I could feel his breath on my face. Our eyes met.

"You see, you are working . . . how should I put it? . . . outside the plan," he said in a barely audible whisper. "Actually, I should keep out of your way, not interfere. On the other hand, it might be better if I give you some . . . that is, if I tell you, in private, of course . . . well, it might avoid needless complications."

"I have nothing to say," I replied, on my guard.

It wasn't the tone of his voice or what he said that gave me hope, but his strikingly unmilitary manner. Unless this was a plan to allay my suspicions, in which case . . .

"I see," he said after a long pause. There was a note of desperation in the voice. He ran a hand through his hair. "Under similar circumstances, on such an assignment . . . every officer would do the same. Yet sometimes, for the sake of the Service of course, one may make an exception . . ."

I looked him in the eye. He winced.

"Very well," I said, taking a seat and resting my fingertips on the desk. "Tell me what you think I ought to know."

"Thank you, thank you! I won't beat around the bush. Your orders come from high up. Now, I am not supposed to know about any change in those orders, not officially. But—well, you know how it is—there are always leaks! Why, you yourself . . ." He waited for some word from me, a sign, a wink, anything. But I sat there like a statue. Finally he blurted out, his face pale and eyes shining feverishly:

"Listen! That old man had been working for *them* for some time. When I unmasked him and he confessed, instead of turning him over to D.S. according to the rules, I decided to keep him in the same position. *They* still considered him their agent, but he was really working for us. One of their couriers was recently sent to meet him, so I laid a trap. Except that instead of the courier, you showed up and . . ." He shrugged.

"Wait a minute! He was working for *us?*"

"Of course! Thanks to me! D.S. would have done the same of course, but that way the matter would have gone out of our hands, I mean my department, though it was I who unmasked him, and someone else would have gotten the credit! Of course, that's not why I did it, don't misunderstand me, I only wanted to expedite matters . . . for the sake of the Service, of course."

"Of course. But why did he—"

"Poison himself? He took you for that courier, he thought you knew about his betrayal. He was only a pawn, after all."

"Yes . . ."

"Yes, it's really quite simple. I went beyond the limits of my authority when I made the decision to keep him. So they sent you to the old man, to get back at me. A typical ploy . . ."

"But wait, I stumbled into that room by accident!"

The officer shook his head and gave a sad smile.

"How could you have known what waited in the other rooms? . . ."

"You mean?—"

His words conjured up an image of a long line of identical old men, each with white hair, pink scalp and gold spectacles, each waiting patiently at his desk, smiling . . . an endless gallery of neat, brightly lit rooms . . . I shuddered.

"Then—it wasn't only in that room?"

"Naturally, we cannot afford to take risks—"

"Then in the other rooms—the same thing?"

He nodded.

"And all those others?"

"Substitutes, of course."

"Working for—?"

"For us, and for them. You know how it is. But we keep a close watch; for us they work harder."

"Wait a minute—what was it the old man was babbling about?—operational plans, millions of variants of the original?"

"A password. You didn't recognize it because it was *their* code; he thought you were pretending not to understand, which would mean you knew all about his defection. After all, everyone wears portable decoders."

He unbuttoned his shirt and showed me a flat device strapped to his chest. Now I remembered how one officer who had talked with me in an elevator suddenly pressed his hand to his heart.

"You mentioned a ploy. Whose ploy?"

He turned pale. The eyelids flickered and fell. For a few minutes he sat with his eyes shut.

"Someone high up," he whispered. "Someone very high up aimed at me, but I swear I am innocent. If you could use your influence and . . ."

"And what?"

"Get them to drop this matter. I would be glad to . . ."

He didn't finish. He made a careful examination of my face. The whites of those staring eyes were wide and glassy. His nervous fingers pulled at his uniform.

"Nine hundred sixty-seven by eighteen by four hundred thirty-nine," he pleaded with me.

I was silent.

"Four hundred, four hundred eleven, six thousand eight hundred ninety-four by three . . . How about it? No? Forty-five? All right, seventy!" He was on his knees, his voice shook. I said nothing. White as a sheet, he got up. "Nine . . . nineteen . . ." One last try. It sounded like a moan. But I said nothing. Slowly, he buttoned his jacket.

"So that's how it is," he said. "I understand. Sixteen. Very well. In accordance with . . . you'll excuse me . . ."

He went to the next room.

"Wait!" I shouted. "You're not going to—?"

A shot, the thud of a body. I froze, my hair stood on end, something urged me to leave at once, to run for my life. There were sounds from the next room, a faint knocking, like a heel tapping the floor, then a rustling—then silence. A dead silence. Through the open door I saw a trouser leg; not taking my eyes off it, I backed towards the exit, groped for the doorknob . . .

The hall was empty. I shut the door, pressed my back against it—there, directly across the hall, standing casually in an open doorway, a fat officer was watching me. My heart skipped a beat. That bored, indifferent expression on his face—it overwhelmed me. He took something out of his pocket—a penknife?—tossed it up and caught it, once, twice, a third time, then held it in his fist, turned his wrist— the blade sprang open with a click. He tested the edge with his thumbnail and grinned. Then he closed his eyes, nodded, stepped back into the room and shut the door. I waited. There was the whine of an elevator, then nothing. I listened to the blood hum in my ears, and I watched the door. Was there someone behind the keyhole?

Cautiously, I started to walk. Once again I was walking alone down endless corridors, corridors that continually branched out and converged, corridors with dazzling walls and rows of white, gleaming doors. I was exhausted, too weak to make another attempt at breaking in somewhere, finding some point of entry into the system. Now and then I leaned against a wall to catch my breath. But they were all too slippery, too perpendicular to rest on. My watch had stopped long ago; I no longer knew whether it was day or night. Sometimes I seemed to fall asleep on my feet, then the slamming of a door somewhere or the whir of a passing elevator would wake me up. I stepped aside for people with briefcases. Now the halls were empty, now they swarmed with officers all heading in the same direction. Work went on around the clock here; one shift left, another took its place. I remember little of the following hours: I was walking, getting on and off elevators, even holding my own in casual conversations—didn't somebody wish me "good night"? But nothing made an impression on me, my mind was like a mirror, or rather like the glazed surface of porcelain.

Then somehow I was outside a bathroom. I entered. Everything was bright and gleaming like an operating room in a hospital. The marble bathtub was like a sarcophagus. I sat down on the edge of it and began to doze. I made one feeble attempt to turn off the blinding light, but there was no switch. The glare from the nickel-plated fixtures was painful, bore into my eyes like fire through the lids, like needles. But I sank into that hard bed, covered my face with an arm, and drifted off. My head struck something sharp, but the pain couldn't wake me.

How long I slept I don't know. It took a while to wake up, to overcome the formless obstacles that haunted my dreams. After a struggle I awoke and was immediately assaulted by a blast of light. A naked bulb hung high on the white ceiling.

My bones felt like they had taken a bad fall. I got up, stripped, had a quick shower. On the wall was a silver dispenser of some fragrant liquid soap, and I found towels embroidered with staring eyes. I dried myself briskly, restoring the circulation, then hurriedly dressed. For the first time in a long time I felt fresh and confident. It was only when my hand touched the door that I remembered where I was. The realization hit me like an electric shock. An endless white labyrinth lay in wait out there, I knew, and an equally endless wandering. The net of corridors, halls and soundproof rooms, each ready to swallow me up . . . the thought made me break out in a cold sweat. For one mad moment I was ready to run out screaming, screaming for help, or for a quick and merciful end. But this weakness passed; I took a deep breath, lifted my head, straightened my clothes, and calmly walked out, my step firm, purposeful, in time to the rhythm of the Building.

I set my watch at eight, picking the hour at random, in order to keep track of at least the relative passage of time. The little-frequented passageway in which I found myself soon led into the usual traffic. Around me the office work continued. I took an elevator down, on the chance it might be breakfast time. But the cafeteria doors were shut; a cleaning crew was at work inside. I turned back and rode up to the third level—the third only because that button looked more worn than the others. The corridor there was empty.

Almost at the very end, just before the turn, a soldier stood guard at a door. His uniform carried no sign of any rank, which was unusual—just a white belt. The soldier held a submachine gun in his gloved hands and stood like a statue. He didn't even blink as I passed. After a few steps I turned back to the door he was guarding: if this was indeed an official entrance to Headquarters, I had little hope of getting in—on the other hand, what was there to lose? I touched the doorknob and glanced at him. He paid no attention, his gaze fixed on the opposite wall. I entered and was amazed to see, straight ahead, a spiral staircase. There was an unusually cold draft. I put out my hand—the chill seemed to come from above, so I started climbing. At the top only the glass of an open door glimmered in the dimness. I found myself on the threshold of a dark chapel. Inside, under a crucifix lay an open coffin. The flickering candles threw little light on the dead man's face. Massive benches stood on either side of the aisle, barely visible in the darkness, and beyond them were niches, their contents altogether hidden. I heard heels clicking on stone but could see no one. I groped up the aisle, pondering my next move, when my eyes happed to fall on the face of the dead man—

it was that little old man! He lay in the casket, covered with a flag that fell to the ground in elaborate folds. His face, serene and waxen, was nestled in starched lace; the spectacles were gone—perhaps that was why his features lacked their former look of alarm and mischief. Now he was quite solemn, as if thoroughly settled, composed. The hands were carefully arranged on either side of the flag, but one little finger had refused to bend with the rest and stuck out in a mocking, or warning gesture. It called attention to itself. From high up came a single note, then a second, with the wheeze and whine of an organ. It sounded as if some passer-by had tried a few notes on the keyboard and then had given up. Again there was silence.

The honors shown the dead man puzzled me; in fact, the whole situation was very odd. I stood at the foot of the casket, my feet freezing, and caught a warm whiff of stearin. A candlewick hissed. Then there was a light tap on my shoulder and a whisper in my ear:

"He's already been searched."

"What?" I blurted out. The word, though certainly not shouted, set up a long and loud echo in the place. A tall officer stood nearby. His face was pale and bloated, his nose blue. A stiff white collar turned back to front shone from under the uniform lapels.

"Did you say something, uh, Father?" I asked. He closed his eyes solemnly, as if to acknowledge my presence as discreetly as possible.

"No, no—a misunderstanding . . . I took you for someone else. Anyway, I'm not a priest, I'm a monk."

"I see."

We stood a while in silence. He lowered his head: it was shaven and covered with a small skullcap.

"Pardon my asking . . . you were acquainted with the deceased?"

"In a way . . . though not very well," I replied. Though all I could see of his eyes were tiny reflections from the candles, it was obvious he was slowly looking me over.

"Paying your last respects?" he whispered with an unpleasant familiarity, and scrutinized me even more closely. I countered with a bold, contemptuous stare. He stiffened.

"You were assigned here then," he sighed. I said nothing.

"There will be Mass," he observed piously. "Obsequies first, then Mass. If you wish . . ."

"It doesn't matter."

"Of course not."

It was growing colder, an icy wind stirred the candles. Then something near the casket caught my eye: a large, heavy air conditioner, churning out freezing air through its metal grating.

"Not a bad arrangement," I remarked. The monk looked quickly over his shoulder and touched my sleeve with an incredibly white, soft hand.

"Permit me to report," he whispered, " . . . many cases of gross negligence, incompetency, conduct not becoming an officer . . . The sergeant prior is not performing his duties . . ."

He said this through his teeth, at the same time watching me closely, ready to retreat at any moment. But I kept silent, my eyes fixed on the shadowy dead man. This lack of response seemed to embolden the monk.

"Of course, it's none of my business . . . I hardly dare," he breathed in my ear. "But if I might ask, in the hope that I could be of some assistance, in the course of duty . . . your orders are from . . . high up?"

"That's right," I said. He grimaced in admiration, exposing large, horsy teeth.

"Permit me—I—I am not disturbing you?"

"Not at all."

"Well . . . you must know that the failures of the Mission are becoming so grave that—"

"You're a missionary?" I asked. He smiled.

"I was speaking of our division, not of our dedication to the Lord."

"Your division?"

"The Theological Division. Quite recently, Father Amnion from the Confidence Section misappropriated . . ."

And he went on. But I lost the thread of what he said—the dead man's little finger, the one that refused to bend with the others, was now moving. The other fingers seemed carved from one piece, like a wax model of a shell, but this one, plumper and pinker than the rest, twitched back and forth, as if to express the slightly rakish character of the deceased. Yet there was something so incorporeal, so fantastically light in that motion, one thought less of resurrection and more of hummingbirds and the kind of tiny insects that appear only in a blur before us. The tremor became more and more pronounced. "Impossible!" I cried. The monk cringed and clutched me.

"You have my sacred word! I speak the truth!"

"What? Oh, I see . . . Well, tell me more," I said, suddenly realizing I preferred his oppressive company to that of the dead man. Besides, the dead man wouldn't dare attempt anything more in the presence of two people.

"The confession files are poorly kept, there's no supervision. At least half of our plants have been spotted. Brother Lieutenant Gatekeeper is extremely careless about giving out passes and writing reports. The Holy Spirit Section has completely neglected provocation activities, angel-baiting . . ."

"You don't say," I muttered. The finger was still. I knew I should leave immediately, but didn't want to be impolite.

"And how is the situation regarding the performance of religious duties?" I threw out, reluctantly playing the role of interrogator—against my better judgment, but at this point I had little choice.

The monk's excitement mounted. The passion of informing was on him. He hissed, his watery eyes glittered, he foamed at the mouth.

"The practice of religious duties!" he said, hoarse with impatience to cast off the heavy weight of accusations he had to make. "The sermons are not effective, attendance is down, the regulations on bugging prayers are generally disregarded. This holds for all denominations, but I speak only of my own. The transgressions in the Higher Goal Section would have led to a scandal; they were hushed up only because Brother Agent Malchus was able to supply the sexton with several willing nuns. And Chaplain Major Orfini, instead of notifying the authorities, plays with mysticism and preaches retribution not of this world."

"You mean, off-planet?"

"If only! Oh no, he—but excuse me, I don't even know your name . . ."

"That's all right."

"Of course . . . now the retribution of Judgment Day, the Apocalypse, that I can understand, thanks mainly to the most efficient methods our scientific colleagues have made possible . . . and then, to make matters worse, Malchus goes around bragging left and right that he's cracked the Bible code! Do you know what that means?"

"Blasphemy?" I offered.

"Blasphemy the Good Lord can take care of, that's no problem. It's our whole order that's at stake, the very theological foundations for the dogma of Divine Desertion!"

"Fine, fine," I said, impatient, "let's skip the theories. This Brother Agent Malchus—what was that all about? Get to the point, Brother."

"As you wish. We've known for a long time that Malchus was a triple agent. The way he said his psalms, you understand . . . Brother Almigens checked him out and we planted a few civilians. For instance, he was seen making certain signs while prostrate before the altar—that in itself constitutes an infraction of paragraph fourteen. Then in the course of the routine quarterly examination we found silver threads sewn into his chasuble."

"Silver threads?"

"What else? For video transmission. I personally conducted an investigation among the communicants."

"Thank you," I said, "that'll do. I get the picture. You may go now, Brother."

"But, but I haven't begun to—"

"Dismissed!"

The monk stood at attention, about-faced, marched off. I was left alone. So . . . religion here was no extracurricular activity, no harmless hobby, but another front for the usual business? The little finger twitched—I reached over and grabbed it, but it broke loose and rolled into a fold in the flag, lying there like a little pink sausage. I picked it up and examined it closely: it was an inflated membrane, the wrinkles and nail painted on in great detail. What sort of prosthetic device was this? Hearing footsteps, I quickly pocketed the object. Several people entered the chapel, carrying a wreath. I retreated behind a column and watched them arrange funeral ribbons with gold letters. A priest appeared at the altar and an acolyte adjusted his vestments. I looked over my shoulder: beneath a bas-relief of Peter Renouncing Christ was a small door. Behind the door I found a narrow passageway that turned to the left. At the end of it, before a large alcove containing a few steps that led to a door, a monk in cowl and sandals sat upon a three-legged stool and turned the pages of his breviary with gnarled fingers. When he lifted his eyes and looked at me, I could see that he was very old. The skullcap sat on his bald head like a patch of mud.

"Where does this go?" I asked, indicating the door.

"Eh?" he croaked, cupping his ear.

"Where does this door lead to?" I shouted, bending over him. A flash of understanding lit his sunken face.

"Nowhere, it don't lead to nowhere . . . It's a cell, Father Marfeon's cell . . . our hermit."

"What?"

"A cell, a cell."

"May I see the hermit then?" I asked. The old monk nodded.

"Yes, this here is our hermitage."

I hesitated, then walked up and opened the door to a dim antechamber cluttered with all sorts of junk—dirty sacks, onion skins, empty jars, sausage rings, ashes and old papers strewn about the floor. Only the center of the room had been swept, or rather, there were a few clean places to put one's foot. I reached the other door, stepping gingerly through the debris, and turned a heavy iron handle. Inside, there was shuffling, whispering. By the light of a single candle somewhere on the floor I saw shadowy figures scurry about, crouch in the corners, scuttle under crooked tables or cots. Someone blew out the candle and there were angry whispers and grunts in the darkness. The air was heavy with the stale smell of unwashed bodies. I beat a hasty retreat. When I passed the old monk, he lifted his eyes from the prayer book.

"Father Marfeon see you?" he rasped.

"He's sleeping," I said, and hurried on. The voice followed me down the hall:

"You come the first time, he's sleeping, but the second time, then you'll see . . ."

I went back through the chapel. The funeral rites were apparently over; the casket, flags and wreaths were gone. Mass too was over. A priest stood in the dim pulpit and admonished the congregation:

". . . for it is written: *And when the devil had ended all the temptation, he departed from him for a season!*" The preacher's shrill voice reverberated beneath the high-domed ceiling: "*For a season* it is written—and where does the devil hide for a season? In that Red Sea that courses through our veins? Or perhaps in Nature? But, O my brothers, are we not ourselves Nature, Nature without end? Does not the rustle of her trees echo in our bones? Is our human blood less salty than the waters of the sea that carve great caverns of lime and chalk, great skeletons beneath the waves? Does not the everlasting fire of the desert burn in our hearts? And are we not, in the end, a clamorous prelude to the final silence, a marriage bed to engender dust, a universe for microbes, microbes that strive to circum-navigate us? We are as unfathomable, as inscrutable as That which brought us into being, and we choke on our own enigma . . ."

"You hear that?" came a whisper behind me. Out of the corner of my eye I saw the sweaty, pale face of a Corporal Brother. "Choking, yet—and that's supposed to be a provocation sermon! He doesn't know how to slip any-thing in!"

"Seek not the key to the mystery, for surely it will never fit! Thou shalt not penetrate the impenetrable! Humble thy-self!" the voice boomed.

"Father Orfini's finished now, I'll call him over. He can be of use, you know—a good man to third-degree!" the pale monk hissed, burning my neck with his foul breath. Some of the worshipers began to turn around and look at us.

"No, don't!" I whispered. Too late—he was already making for the altar by a side passage. I tried to leave unobtrusively, but the exit was too crowded; the monk was already returning with the priest (now back in uniform), pulling him by the sleeve. Then with a conspiratorial wink he disappeared behind a column, leaving the priest and me alone in the empty chapel.

"You wish to make confession, my son?" he asked in a melodious voice, presenting me with the stern face of an ascetic, gray at the temples, and with a gold tooth. The gold reminded me of the little old man.

"No, that's all right," I said. Then a thought occurred to me, and I added:

"I am in need of certain . . . information."

The father confessor nodded.

"Very well, follow me."

Behind the altar was a low door, which led into an al-most black corridor. On each side stood the robed figures of saints, their faces turned to the wall. We entered a painfully bright room with an enormous safe, a black enamel cross inlaid on its stainless steel. The priest offered me a chair and went over to a table cluttered with old papers and books. Even in uniform he looked very much a priest: the white, expressive hands like those of a concert pianist, the delicate blue veins about the forehead, the dry skin that stretched across the bones. Everything about him bespoke a stern serenity.

"Go ahead," he said.

"Do you know the man in charge of the Department of Instructions?" I asked. His eyebrows lifted slightly.

"Major Erms? Yes, I know him."

"And the number of his office?"

The priest became confused; he fingered the buttons of his uniform as if it were a cassock.

"Did anything—" he began, but I interrupted.

"Now Father, let's have the number."

"Nine thousand one hundred twenty-nine . . . but I don't understand why I—"

"Nine thousand one hundred twenty-nine," I repeated slowly, certain that this was one number I would not forget.

The priest was clearly taken aback.

"Excuse me, I . . . Brother Persuasion gave me to understand that—"

"Brother Persuasion? The monk who brought you over to me? What's your opinion of him, Father?"

"I really don't know what you mean," the priest said, still standing behind his desk. "Brother Persuasion heads our Handicrafts Unit."

"Handicrafts?"

"Ecclesiastical attire, vestments, pontificals, various liturgical paraphernalia, aspergers, thuribles, censers, etc."

"That's all?"

"Well, on special order . . . for Department S.D. I believe we made a number of bugged percolators, and I know our Gerontophile Section produces earmuffs and miscellaneous items for our suffering senior citizens, for example polygraph mittens."

"Polygraph mittens?"

"The galvanic skin response, you know—records their hidden moments of excitement . . . Then there are microphone pillows for those who talk in their sleep, and so on. But, you couldn't tell me . . .? Did Brother Persuasion . . . say anything about me?"

"He spoke of various things . . ." I let it hang there.

"The people in the Department?"

"You might say . . ."

"One moment, please."

The priest hurried to the safe and in three quick motions opened the combination lock. The steel door swung aside with a clang, revealing stacks of sealed folders in all colors. These he feverishly searched—then pounced on one. His face was covered with tiny beads of sweat.

"Make yourself at home, I'll be right back."

"Oh no you don't!" I yelled, jumping up. "Hand over that folder!"

I did this on the spur of the moment.

He clutched the folder to his chest. I looked him in the eye and grabbed an edge of it. He wouldn't let go.

"Nineteen," I said slowly. A drop of sweat ran down his cheek like a tear. The folder eased itself into my hands. I opened it—it was empty.

"My duty . . . I acted under orders . . . from high up," the priest muttered.

"Sixteen," I said.

"No! Anything but that!!"

"Be seated, Father. You will not leave this room until you are given the proper authorization by phone. Is that understood?"

"Yes! Yes!"

"Nor will you initiate any calls yourself, Father!"

"I won't! I swear!"

"Good."

I left and closed the door, went back through the chapel and down the spiral staircase. This time there was no guard at the entrance. In the elevator I noticed that the yellow folder taken from the priest was still in my hand.

Room 9129 was on the ninth level, sure enough. I entered without knocking.

One of the secretaries was knitting, the other worked on a ham sandwich and a cup of coffee. I looked for a door to the chief's office. There wasn't any, which was odd.

"Major Erms, Special Mission," I announced. The secretaries acted as if they hadn't heard me. The one who was knitting counted stitches under her breath. A code? I examined the small room more carefully: rows of bookshelves on every wall, bookshelves and file cabinets, a microphone painted like a flower and hanging above one shelf at an unusual height. Without another word, I placed my yellow folder on the desk in front of the girl with the ham sandwich. She glanced at it, chewing. Pale pink gums showed above her teeth. With the little finger of her left hand she pushed back the wax paper that held her sandwich. A secret sign? I walked along the shelves and noticed a gap between two cabinets . . . something white . . . a door. There was a door behind one of the bookshelves. I gripped the shelf and pulled hard. The files above my head swayed dangerously.

"Sixteen . . . *nineteen*," the knitting secretary counted in a whisper that became suddenly shrill. The shelf caught on something halfway—but I had access to the door and managed to turn the knob and squeeze through.

4

"So you decided to show up at last!" a young, vibrant voice greeted me. A blond officer got up from behind his mahogany desk. The room was stifling hot and he was in his shirtsleeves. "You're a little dirty from the wall . . ."

He took out a small brush and applied it to the sleeve of my jacket as he talked.

"I expected you yesterday. You will be able to spend the night, won't you? My work kept me in the office all day, but at least this way I couldn't miss you. There, now you look fine. You know, I've become so familiar with your case that here I am treating you like an old friend and we haven't even been introduced! I'm Erms."

"And you have my instructions," I said.

"Why else would I be here? Coffee?"

"Thanks."

He poured me a cup, threw the brush in a drawer and took a seat. The smile never left his face. He had the winsome air of a towheaded boy, though when I looked closer I saw wrinkles around those bright blue eyes—laugh lines, no doubt. His teeth were like a puppy's, clean and sharp.

"Okay, down to business. Your instructions. Now let's see, where did I put them . . ."

"Just don't tell me you have to leave the room to get them," I said with a strained smile. This sent him into such gales of laughter that the tears streamed from his eyes. He had to loosen his tie.

"Terrific! What a clown! But I really don't have to go anywhere to get them, they're right here." And he went over to a small safe, took out a thick bundle of papers and tossed it on the desk. "No use kidding you, the Old Boy gave you a tough nut to crack. It won't be any picnic. And it's your first, isn't it?"

"That's right," I admitted, then added, since he seemed such a decent guy: "You know, if I stayed around here long enough, I could become a pro at this game without actually going on a single mission. I mean, it's in the air . . . you take it in, you absorb the . . . the . . ." I couldn't find the right word.

"The local color!" he said and again broke into loud laughter. I laughed too, feeling light and happy as I stirred my coffee. Yet there was some unpleasant association connected with this stirring, something recent. I couldn't remember . . .

"May I see my instructions?" I asked.

"They're all yours."

He pushed the bundle to me across the desk.

"Just a second," he said in a low voice, gentle but insistent, just as I began to read. "Perhaps we should first take care of certain—formalities. An ugly, bureaucratic term, I know, but . . . you'll cooperate, won't you?"

"Formalities?" I had a sinking feeling.

"Isn't there a call you ought to make? . . ." he suggested discreetly.

"Of course, I completely forgot! That priest in the Theological Department. May I use your phone?"

"Don't bother, I already took care of that for you."

"You did? But how—"

"Forget it, it's nothing. But wasn't there something else—?"

"I can't think of anything . . . Unless you want me to make a report."

"If you like, but I don't insist."

"Major Erms, was this whole thing—a test?"

"A test?"

"Oh, some sort of entrance exam. I mean, the abilities of a novice might be questioned, so they might want to, you know, set up certain situations . . ."

"Really!" Apparently I had hurt his feelings; he sounded injured, grieved. "Tests? Entrance exams? Setting up situations? How can you think of such a thing? No, what I had in mind was . . . you took something there, didn't you? Something for me? Tsk-tsk, how absentminded!" My confusion amused him. "Come now, it was in the chapel . . . you have it with you, it's right in your pocket, isn't it?"

"Oh, *that!*"

I pulled out the painted membrane finger and handed it over.

"Fine," he said. "This will be added to the evidence against him."

"What's in it?" I asked.

He raised the pink sausage to the light. It was empty, like a balloon.

"Proof of ostentation—a damaging entry in his dossier."

"The old man?"

"Of course."

"But he's dead."

"So? It was clearly a hostile act. You were a witness! Right there, on the flag—"

"But he's dead!"

He chuckled.

"My dear boy, wouldn't we be in fine shape if death excused everything! But enough of that. I want to thank you for your cooperation. Now let's get back to business. Before you start out we have to go through some things."

"What exactly?"

"Oh, nothing unpleasant, I assure you. Routine induction. Propaedeutics. Are you familiar, for example, with the basic codes you'll have to use?"

"No, I guess not."

"You see? Now, there are calling codes, stalling codes, departmental codes, special codes, and—you'll like this," he grinned, "they're changed every day. A necessary precaution, but what a bother! Each section, of course, has its own system, so the same word or name will have different meanings on different levels."

"Even names?"

"Sure. If you could only see the look on your face!" He laughed. "Take the official name of our Commander in Chief, for example. Haven't you noticed that all the names of his staff have a certain ring to them?"

"True . . ."

"There, you see?"

He grew serious.

"Grade, rank, even greetings, everything is coded."

"Greetings?"

"Certainly. Suppose you're talking with someone over the phone, someone on the outside, and you say, for instance, 'Good evening.' From that alone one can deduce that our work goes on at night, that there are shifts in other words, which is important information—for someone," he stressed the last word. "Every conversation . . ."

"Wait! You mean, even now . . ."

He cleared his throat, embarrassed.

"Unavoidable."

"Then how am I to understand . . .?"

He looked straight at me.

"Why do you say that?" he said, lowering his voice. "Of course you understand, you must. *Completely forgot, Can't think of anything, Some sort of entrance exam*—how could you *not* understand? But I can see that you do! Now why that look of despair? Each one codes according to his ability and mission. Don't worry, you'll catch on soon enough."

"If you say so."

"Have a little confidence in yourself! Business is business, I know, the impersonal routine, the complications, frustrations . . . yet your mission is so fantastically difficult that it's silly to let a few little mistakes discourage you, even if they *are* irreparable. I'll direct you to the Department of Codes, they'll tell you everything you need to know—nothing rigorous, you understand, just enough to handle a social conversation. And the instructions will be waiting for you here."

"I didn't even get a chance to look at them."

"No one's stopping you."

I opened the bundle and glanced at the top of the first page:

". . . You won't be able to find the right room—none of them will have the number designated on your pass. First you will wind up at the Department of Verification, then the Department of Misinformation, then some clerk from the Pressure Section will advise you to try level eight, but on level eight they will ignore you . . ."

I skipped a few pages and read:

". . . you will have suspected for some time now that the Cosmic Command, obviously no longer able to supervise every assignment on an individual basis when there are literally trillions of matters in its charge, has switched over to a random system. The assumption will be that every document, circulating endlessly from desk to desk, must eventually hit upon the right one."

"What—what is this?" I stammered, looking up at Major Erms, paralyzed by a sudden stab of fear.

"Code," he answered absently, searching for something in his desk. "Instructions have to be in code."

"But—but this sounds like . . ." I couldn't finish.

"Code should sound like anything but code."

Reaching across the desk, he lifted the instructions from my hands.

"I couldn't . . . take them with me?"

"Whatever for?"

His voice registered genuine surprise.

"They could help me decipher them in that—that Department of Codes," I said.

He laughed.

"What an amateur! But you'll learn. After a while these things become second nature. Look, how could you allow your instructions to end up in anyone else's hands? Remember, only three people know about your Mission: the Commander in Chief, the Chief Commander, and myself."

I watched meekly as he put the bundle back inside the safe and spun the combination dials a few times.

"But at least tell me what my Mission is about," I urged. "Give me a rough idea."

"A rough idea?" He bit his lip; an unruly shock of hair fell into his left eye. He leaned against the desk with his fingertips, whistled softly like a schoolboy, then heaved a sigh and smiled. There was a dimple in his left cheek.

"What on earth am I going to do with you?" He shrugged, went back to the safe, took out the same bundle and asked:

"You have a folder, I believe? We'll stuff the lot in there."

The empty yellow folder I brought with me but had left outside now turned up on his desk, and he filled it with my instructions.

"There you are," he said, handing it over with a broad grin. "Your instructions—and in a yellow folder, yet!"

"The color signifies something?"

My innocence amused him.

"Does it signify something, he asks. That's great! But no more jokes, let's be off. I'll show you the way . . ."

I hurried after him, holding the heavy folder tightly under my arm. We went through an office as large and long as a classroom. On the walls above the heads of the clerical staff were blueprints of aqueducts and dams, and above those, almost at the ceiling, huge maps of the Red Planet —I recognized the canals at once. Major Erms opened a door for me and we passed between rows of desks. No one looked up from his work. Another room: an enormous chart representing the body of a rat, and rat skeletons in glass cages, looking like empty walnuts tied together with wire. The walls curved. Around the bend several people peered into microscopes, each surrounded by slides, tweezers, jars of glue. Farther on, people were ironing out and meticulously assembling tiny bits of dirty paper. There was a sharp smell of chlorine in the air.

"By the way," said Major Erms in a confidential whisper

when we were walking alone down a white corridor, "if you ever need to throw anything away—an unimportant document, a note, or a rough draft of something—never use the toilet for that purpose. It only makes unnecessary work for our people."

"How come?" I asked. He frowned impatiently.

"Must everything be spelled out for you? That was the Department of Sanitation we just passed. I use it as a shortcut. All our drainpipes are monitored, the sewage carefully filtered, every bit of it, before it can be cleared. These are, after all, roads to the outside, hence potential information leaks. Ah, our elevator."

It opened and an officer in a trench coat stepped out with a violin case tucked under his arm. He asked us if we would mind waiting while he moved his packages off the elevator. Suddenly there was a loud bang, quite close—he leaped from the elevator, tossed his packages at us and dashed up the corridor, frantically opening the violin case. One package caught me in the chest and I fell back against the closing elevator door. The chatter of an automatic began around the corner; something cracked overhead and a cloud of chalky dust came down the walls.

"Down! Down!" yelled Major Erms, pulling my arm. We hit the floor together. The corridor thundered from one end to the other, bullets whined above our heads, plaster sprinkled down. The officer fell, his violin case flew open— confetti came swirling out like snow. The smell of gunpowder seared our nostrils. A small capsule was pressed into my hand.

"When I give the signal, put that between your teeth and bite!" Major Erms shouted in my ear. Someone was running.

A deafening explosion. Major Erms pulled out several envelopes, stuffed them in his mouth and chewed like mad, spitting out stamps as if they were pits. Another explosion, a grenade.

The fallen officer gave the death rattle, his left leg beat

against the hard floor. Erms counted the kicks, got up on his elbows—and gave a cheer:

"Two plus five! We won!" He sprang to his feet, dusted himself off and handed me the folder. "Come on, we'll try to get you some meal tickets."

"What was all that about?" I gasped, still shaken.

The dying man kicked the floor twice, five times, twice, five times . . .

"That? An unmasking."

"And . . . now we just leave?"

"Sure. This," he pointed to the twitching body. "is not our Department."

"But—"

"Section Seven will take care of him. There, you see? Here come the Theologicals."

A chaplain approached, preceded by an altar boy ringing a Sanctus bell. As we entered the elevator, I could still hear the dying man's coded agony. At the tenth level Major Erms held out his hand instead of getting off.

"Well?"

"Well what?"

"The capsule."

"Oh. Here it is."

I was clutching it in my hand. He put it in a wallet.

"What was it?"

"Nothing."

He let me out first, and we headed for the nearest door. A fat officer sat by a table in a perfectly square room, munching candy from a paper bag. Other than that, there was only a very small black door, barely large enough for even a child.

"Where's Prandtl?" asked Major Erms. The fat officer, still chewing, held up three fingers. His uniform was unbuttoned. He seemed to pour out over his chair. The face was bloated, the neck full of folds, and he wheezed terribly when he breathed.

"Good," said Major Erms. "Prandtl will be here any

minute. Make yourself at home, he'll take good care of you. And whenever you have a free moment, drop in for those meal tickets. Be seeing you!"

After he left, I took a seat by the wall and watched the fat man. The candy crunched in his teeth, the lips smacked. I looked away, afraid he might have a stroke right before my eyes—the skin around his neck was awfully blue, and his breathing came in great, tortured gasps. But this was apparently normal for the fat man; he hardly seemed to notice. He fought for breath, he munched candy. I wanted to grab the paper bag from his hands. He stuffed himself, one candy after another, swallowing hard, turning red, then purple; the sticky fingers reached for another. I looked away, but I couldn't turn my back on him altogether—I was afraid he might choke to death behind my back, and I didn't want a corpse behind me. I closed my eyes and tried to think.

Had my situation improved or not? Apparently it had. But then there were so many *but*'s. For instance, Major Erms had been quite prepared to poison me (I had no doubts about the contents of that capsule). Then there was the little old man in the gold spectacles—chances were I wasn't free of him yet. But my big worry was the instructions. They duplicated to the letter my every step inside the Building—more, my every thought! This indicated I was still under observation, though Erms had vehemently denied that—however, he later admitted that our conversation was not to be taken literally, that everything was in code, an allusion to other meanings, hidden meanings, meanings on different levels. But this was not what really bothered me. *I was beginning to doubt the very existence of the instructions themselves.* Of course, that was utter nonsense. Why would they observe me and subject me to all these tests if I were not on a Special Mission, if I were not of great importance to them? Clearly, I was no earthly use to anyone without this assignment, this assignment which had come so unexpectedly, so mysteriously, and which they sometimes suspended, sometimes half-heartedly confirmed.

If I could ask them one question, just one question, it would be: "What do you want me to do?"

And any answer would be welcome, any answer at all . . . except one . . .

The fat officer startled me with a loud snort. He blew his nose and examined the handkerchief carefully before folding it and putting it away.

The door opened and a tall, gaunt officer walked in. Something about him—I couldn't quite put my finger on it —gave the impression of a civilian disguised in a uniform. He took off his glasses and twirled them as he approached.

"You wanted to see me?"

"Mr. Prandtl from the Department of Codes?" I asked, getting up.

"Except that I'm a captain. Remain seated. Interested in codes, eh?"

The last syllable was aimed like a shot between my eyes.

"Yes, Captain."

"Don't call me Captain. Coffee?"

"Please."

The small black door swung open and a hand placed a tray with two cups of coffee before us. Prandtl put on his glasses and his features froze into a hard, fierce expression.

"Define code," he snapped like a hammer on metal.

"Code is a system of signs which can be translated into ordinary language with the help of a key."

"The smell of a rose—code or not?"

"Not a code, because it is not a sign for anything; it is merely itself, a smell. Only if it were used to signify something else could we consider it a code."

I was glad of this opportunity to demonstrate my ability to think logically. The fat officer leaned over in my direction until his buttons began to pop. I ignored him. Prandtl took off his glasses and smiled.

"The rose, does it smell just because, or for a reason?"

"It attracts bees with its smell, the bees pollinate it . . ."

He nodded.

"Precisely. Now let's generalize. The eye converts a light wave into a neural code, which the brain must decipher. And the light wave, from where does it come? A lamp? A star? That information lies in its structure; it can be read."

"But that's not a code," I interrupted. "A star or a lamp doesn't attempt to conceal information, which is the whole purpose of a code."

"Oh?"

"Obviously! It all depends on the intention of the sender."

I reached for my coffee. A fly was floating in it. Had the fat officer planted it there? I glanced at him: he was picking his nose. I fished the fly out with my spoon and let it drop on the saucer. It clinked—metal, sure enough.

"The intention?" Prandtl put on his glasses. The fat officer (I was keeping an eye on him) began to rummage through his pockets, wheezing so violently that his face moved like a bunch of balloons. It was revolting.

"Take a light wave," Prandtl continued, "emitted by a star. What kind of star? Big or little? Hot or cold? What's its history, its future, its chemical composition? Can we or can we not tell all this from its light?"

"We can, with the proper know-how."

"And the proper know-how?"

"Yes?"

"That's the key, isn't it?"

"Still," I said carefully, "light is not code."

"It isn't?"

"The information it carries wasn't hidden there. And besides, using your argument, we'd have to conclude that everything is code."

"And so it is, absolutely everything. Code or camouflage. Yourself included."

"You're joking."

"Not at all."

"I'm a code?"

"Or a camouflage. Every code is a camouflage, not every camouflage is a code."

"Perhaps," I said, following it through, "if you are thinking about genetics, heredity, those programs of ourselves we carry around in every cell . . . In that way I am a code for my progeny, my descendants. But camouflage? What would I have to do with camouflage."

"You," Prandtl replied drily, "are not in my jurisdiction."

He went over to the small black door. A hand appeared with a piece of paper, which he turned over to me.

"THREAT OUTFLANKING MANEUVER STOP," it read, "REINFORCEMENTS SECTOR SEVEN NINE FOUR HUNDRED THIRTY-ONE STOP QUARTERMASTER SEVENTH OPERATIONAL GROUP GANZMIRST COL DIPL STOP."

I looked up—another fly was floating in my coffee. The fat officer yawned.

"Well?" asked Prandtl. His voice seemed far away. I pulled myself together.

"A telegram, a deciphered telegram."

"No. It's in code, we have yet to crack it."

"But it looks like—"

"Camouflage," he said. "They used to camouflage codes as innocent information, private letters, poems, etc. Now each side tries to make the other believe that the message isn't coded at all. You follow?"

"I guess."

"Now here's the text run through our D.E.C. machine."

He went back to the small black door, pulled a piece of paper from the fingers there and gave it to me.

"BABIRUSANTOSITORY IMPECLANCYBILLISTIC MATOTEOSIS AIN'T CATACYPTICALLY AMBREGATORY NOR PHAROGRANTOGRAPHICALLY OSCILLUMPTUOUS BY RETROVECTACALCIPHICATION NEITHER," I read and stared at him.

"That's deciphered?"

He smiled tolerantly.

"The second stage," he explained. "The code was designed to yield gibberish upon any attempt to crack it. This is to convince us that the telegram wasn't coded in the first place, that the original message can be taken at face value."

"But it can't?" He nodded.

"Watch. I'll run it through again."

A piece of paper dropped from the hand in the small black door. Something red moved around inside. But Prandtl got in the way so I couldn't see. I picked up the paper—it was still warm, either from the hand or from the machine.

"ABRUPTIVE CELERATION OF ALL DERVISHES CARRYING BIBUGGISH PYRITES VIA TURMAND HIGHLY RECOMMENDED."

That was the text. I shook my head.

"Now what?" I asked.

"The machine has done what it can. Now we take over." And he yelled, "Kruuh!"

"Huh?" the fat officer groaned, suddenly jolted from his stupor. He turned his bleary eyes to Prandtl. Prandtl bellowed:

"Abruptive celeration!"

"Therrr . . ." croaked the fat officer.

"All dervishes!"

"Weeee! Beeee!" he bleated.

"Bibuggish pyrites!"

"Naaaa! Waaaa!"

"Turmand!"

"Saa . . . serr . . ." Saliva trickled down his chin. "Waa . . . wan . . . serr . . . rrr . . . Grrr! Growl! Ho ho ho! Ha ha ha!" He broke into wild laughter which ended in a fit of horrible gurgling. The face turned deep purple, tears streamed down his cheeks and jowls, the massive body was racked with sobs.

"Enough, Kruuh! Enough!!" yelled Prandtl. "An error," he said, turning to me. "False association. But you still heard the entire text."

"Text? What text?"

"*There will be no answer.*" The fat officer sat back in his chair, trembling. Little by little he quieted down and, moaning softly to himself, caressed his face with both hands, as if to comfort it.

"There will be no answer?" I repeated. Hadn't I heard those words recently? But where? "Is that all it says?" I asked Prandtl. He gave a twisted smile.

"If I were to show you a text richer in meaning, we might both regret it later on. Even so . . ."

"Even so?!" I flared up, as if that careless remark somehow concerned me vitally. Prandtl shrugged.

"This was a sample of our latest code, not too complicated, in multiple camouflage."

He was clearly trying to divert my attention from that slip. I wanted to get back to it, but all I could say was:

"According to you, everything is code."

"Correct."

"In that case, every text? . . ."

"Yes."

"A literary text?"

"Certainly. Come with me." He motioned me over to the small black door. There was no other room inside, only the dark surface of a machine, a small keyboard, a nickel-plated slot from which a piece of printout tape curled like a reptile tongue.

"Give me a line from some literary work," Prandtl said, turning to me.

"Shakespeare?"

"Whatever you like."

"You maintain that his plays are nothing but coded messages?"

"Depends what you mean by a coded message. But let's give it a try, shall we?"

I tried to think, but nothing came to me except Othello's "Excellent wretch!" That seemed a bit brief and inappropriate.

"I've got it!" I announced with sudden inspiration. *"My ears have not yet drunk a hundred words of that tongue's utterance, yet I know the sound: Art thou not Romeo and a Montague?"*

"Fine."

Prandtl had hardly typed this out when the tape began to move from the slot, a paper snake. He gently handed the end of it to me, and I waited patiently while the printout emerged. The vibration of the machine suddenly stopped and the rest of the tape came out blank. I read:

"BAS TARD MATT HEWS VAR LET MATT HEWS SCUM WOULD BASH THAT FLAP EAR ASS WITH PLEA SURE GREAT THAT MATT HEWS BAS"

"What's this?" I asked, perplexed. Prandtl gave a knowing nod.

"Shakespeare evidently harbored a grudge against someone by the name of Matthews and chose to put this in code when he wrote those lines."

"What? You mean, he deliberately used that beautiful scene to disguise a lot of foul language directed at some Matthews?"

"Who says he did it deliberately? A code is a code, regardless of the author's intention."

"Let's see something," I said, and typed the decoded text into the machine myself. The tape moved again, spiraling onto the floor. Prandtl smiled but said nothing.

"IF ONLY SHE'D GIVE ME TRA LA LA TRA LA LA IF ONLY TRA LA LA SHE'D GIVE ME LA LA, TRA LA LA AND GIVE ME TRA LA LA HA HA HA TRA LA LA," went the letters of the printout.

"Now what do you make of it?"

"We have moved deeper into the seventeenth-century Englishman's psyche."

"Are you trying to tell me that Shakespeare's great poetry is nothing but bastard Matthews and tra la la? At that rate, your machine will reduce our monuments of literature, creations of genius, immortal works, all to complete gibberish!"

"Precisely," answered Prandtl. "Gibberish. The arts, literature, what is their true purpose? Diversion!"

"Diversion from what?"

"You don't know?"

"No."

"You should."

I was silent.

"A cracked code remains a code. An expert can peel away layer after layer. It's inexhaustible. One digs ever deeper into more and more inaccessible strata. That journey has no end."

"How can this be? What about 'There will be no answer'—didn't you say that was the final result?"

"No. It was only a stage. Real enough, within the framework of those proceedings, but a stage nonetheless. Give it some thought; you'll come to the same conclusion."

"I don't understand."

"You will, in good time. Yet even that will be but another stage."

"Couldn't you help me a little?"

"You're on your own, as everyone is. It's tough, to be sure —but you've been singled out, you know the score. We're out of time now. In the future I'll do what I can for you. In the line of duty, of course."

"But how . . . I still don't know—" I said in alarm. "Weren't you supposed to brief me on the codes for the Mission?"

"Mission?"

"Yes."

"Specify it."

"I . . . I don't have the details, I assume it's all spelled out in my instructions. Here they are, in this folder. Of course, I'm not allowed to show you—hold on, where's my folder?"

I jumped up, looked under the table—the folder was

gone! The fat officer, bloated and gaping like a dead fish, snored heavily on his seat.

"Where's my folder?!" I shouted in his ear.

"Easy," Prandtl said behind my back. "Nothing gets lost here. Kruuh! Kruuh!!" he scolded. "Give it back! Do you hear, give it back!"

The fat officer shifted his weight and something fell to the floor—my folder. I grabbed it, checked to see if it was still full.

Had he been sitting on it, then? If he swiped it right from under my nose, he was more dexterous than he looked. I was about to open the folder when I remembered that I couldn't read my instructions properly without the key, and Prandtl couldn't give me the key unless he knew what they were about. A vicious circle. I explained it to him.

"Probably an oversight on Major Erms's part," I concluded.

"Who knows?" he said.

"I'll check it out!" I said, challenging him. In other words: I'll go to him and tell him you are washing your hands of the whole affair, you are sabotaging my Mission, a Mission assigned by the Commander in Chief himself!

"Do whatever you think is right," he said, then added with a shade of hesitation: "But . . . are you sure you know the proper procedure?"

"The same procedure that has me leave here empty-handed?" I asked coolly.

Prandtl took off his glasses. His face, as if suddenly unmasked, assumed a look of weary helplessness. I sensed that he wanted to tell me something, but couldn't—or wasn't allowed. The hostility which had been mounting between us was suddenly dispelled. I began to feel sympathy for this man.

"You . . . you're acting under orders?" he asked in such a small voice that I could hardly hear him.

"Under orders? . . . I guess."

"I am too."

He opened the door and stood there like a statue, waiting for me to leave. As I passed him, his lips parted, but the word remained unspoken. He only sighed, stepped back and slammed the door in my face. Once again I found myself in the corridor, clutching my folder. But if my visit to the Department of Codes had not brought the desired results—that is, to tell me something of my Mission—at least this time I had a destination. That in itself was something. I repeated the number to myself: 9129. I would ask Major Erms for the meal tickets he promised me. A good pretext . . .

I passed several white doors before I remembered the folder. If my instructions (I had to assume they existed) continued in the vein of the excerpts I had read in Major Erms's office, then they would trace all my future movements through the Building. A staggering thought, that. And yet wherever I went there were indications that others knew more about my aimless wanderings from room to room than I myself. Could it be that the folder really held a complete itinerary of my journey, including what lay in store for me at its conclusion? The few lines I already read certainly suggested that possibility; even my innermost thoughts had been accurately recorded.

I decided to open the folder, wondering only why I hadn't done that before. If I indeed held my fate in my own two hands, why not take a peek?

5

The row of doors on my right came to a sudden end. Most likely, there was a very long room on the other side of the wall. A little farther along I found a corridor which led to a bathroom. The door was open, so I peeked in: the coast was clear. I locked myself in and took a seat on the edge of the tub, then noticed a small, dark object on the shelf under the mirror—a straight razor placed invitingly on a clean hand towel. It bothered me for some reason. I picked it up; it looked brand new. Everything gleamed here with the dazzling cleanliness of an operating room. I put the razor back. Somehow I just couldn't bring myself to open the folder here. I left the bathroom and took the elevator to the level below, to the same bathroom where I had stayed the night before.

This one was empty too and exactly as I had left it, except that the towels were new. I sat on the edge of the tub, untied the folder and pulled out a thick stack of paper.

The pages were blank, all of them. A senseless, wild rattling ran through the pipes, the sort of noise that accompanies the opening of a tap on another floor. It moaned with an almost human voice, then gurgled and faded as it traveled out in the cast-iron intestines of the Building. My hands trembled as I turned the white sheets over, one by one; I counted them mechanically, pointlessly. It was Prandtl—no, it was that fat officer! I'd beat that swollen swine to a pulp, so help me!

My anger passed as quickly as it had come. Of course the whole thing had been planned, carefully planned. But why steal my instructions? All Major Erms had to do was not give them to me in the first place.

But wait, there was something here, hidden between all

these blank pages—a layout of the Building, with a map of the mountain that contained the Building, and attached to this, sewn on with white thread, a twelve-point plan, "Operation Shovel." Of course, I would have to turn this over to the authorities, explain how it came into my possession. But would they believe me? How could I prove I hadn't familiarized myself with this classified material? That I hadn't committed the Building's location to memory—one hundred and eighteen miles south of Mount Harvurd—or the layout of the Building for that matter, or the position of Headquarters for the Chiefs of Staff? No, I hadn't a prayer. Now I began to see a pattern to the events of the past four days: all those accidental, unrelated incidents had actually been weaving an intricate net to pull me ever deeper, ever closer to this moment of truth.

How I longed to tear those compromising documents to shreds and flush them down the toilet forever! But I remembered Major Erms's caution. How true it was that nothing happened here by chance! Every word, every move of the head, the least expression, the most absentminded gesture—everything was by design, part of an enormous machine that was obviously bent on my destruction! I felt as if I were surrounded by a million brightly shining eyes. If only there were someplace to hide, a crevice, a ledge, if only I could vanish into air, cease to exist . . . The razor! Is *that* why it was there? They knew I would want to be alone, they placed it there on purpose . . .

Automatically, I put the papers back in the folder one by one. As the folder gradually filled, so my mind was gradually emptied of its ideas, its hopes to find some way out, to hit on some bold stratagem, some trump card. More and more I could see before me the image of my own face, the cringing, sweaty face of a condemned man. I was defeated, destroyed—what more was there to lose? That simple thought emerged from the multitude of my wild, desperate schemes as a kind of salvation.

As I was preparing to accept the thorny crown of a

martyr, an index card slipped out and dropped at my feet. There was a number on it, almost illegible—3883—and now I saw that someone had printed in "Rm" before the number, evidently a precaution to make the message clear. Or was it an order?

So be it! I picked up my folder and took a last look around. There was my face in the mirror, watching me as if through a dark and broken window. Broken because of the flaws in the glass, or was I seeing myself through the prism of fear? We observed one another, myself and I. So that's how it looked to be a traitor! This ugly face, bathed in sweat and twisted in fear, would soon cease to exist. The thought was almost pleasant. Ah, but I had known all along that it would come to this!

Yes, there was something to savor in this bowing to the inevitable . . . But wait, what if I were to misplace these papers? Then I would be left with nothing, not even a Mission, not even my betrayal . . . Was I caught in the machinery of some giant conspiracy, ground in the gears of some struggle between two opposing forces? If that were indeed the case, some higher authority might yet intercede on my behalf.

Room 3883, I decided, would be the last resort. In the meantime there was Prandtl. Whatever the true situation was, he did sigh in my face. That signified something. He *sighed*—he was on my *side*. True, he had distracted me while the fat officer stole my instructions. Orders were orders. He admitted he was acting under orders.

The corridor was empty on the way to Prandtl. I went very slowly. Something seemed to be holding me back. When I entered the office at last, no one was in. There were two cups on the table. Mine was the one with the metal flies in the saucer: they lay there like two pits. The desk near the wall was cluttered with various documents. I went over and picked through them on the off chance that at least some of my instructions might have found their way there. I did find a yellow folder, but it contained only the payroll, a list of curious specialties: Infernalist, Counterinformant First Class, Top Envelope Macerator, Undercover Perjurer, Master Cremator and Osteophage Provocateur . . . The phone suddenly rang with an urgency that made me jump. I lifted the receiver.

"Hello?" came a masculine voice. "Hello?"

Before I could reply, someone else hooked up on the line. I could hear both voices.

"It's me," said the first voice. "We have a problem, Captain!"

"He's in trouble, eh?"

"We're afraid he might do something to himself."

"Weak, eh? I'm not surprised."

"He's all right, really, but you know what can happen. We need to keep the lid on this—"

"That's up to Six, not me."

"Can't you do anything?"

"For him? Not a thing, not a blessed thing . . ."

I listened with bated breath; the suspicion that they were talking about me was becoming a certainty. There was a pause.

"You're sure?"

"Take it up with Six."

"That means retiring him from the assignment."

"So?"

"Then we have to give him up?"

"You don't want to, eh?"

"It's not a matter of what I want, sir—it's just that, well, he's become accustomed to—"

"Look, you have your own specialists there, don't you? What does Prandtl say?"

"Prandtl? Nothing, not since the parting sigh. Anyway, he's at a meeting."

"Have him paged. I mean it, I refuse to have anything to do with this business."

"I'll send him operatives from the Medical Department."

"Suit yourself. I have to go now. That'll be all."

"Yes, sir."

They both hung up and I was left with a soft whispering in my ear, as if the receiver were a sea shell. Were they talking about me or not?

At least I had learned that Prandtl was at a meeting. There were footsteps, someone was coming from the next room. I ran out into the corridor, hesitated—but I could hardly go back now. No, now it was a choice between Major Erms and Room 3883. Room 3883 had to be somewhere on the third level. The Department of Investigation? Once there, you never leave ... Then again, walking up and down the corridors was not so bad, really. I could rest in an elevator, stand around, hide in the bathroom ...

The razor. Strange I hadn't thought of it till now. Meant for me? Perhaps. But I was too agitated to think that through. I took the staircase down, feeling dizzy. The fifth level. The fourth. Third. The corridor was white, extremely clean and straight—3887, 3886, 3885, 3884, 3883. My heart in my throat, I resolved to take a peek inside. If anybody would ask, I could say I was looking for Major Erms and happened to open the wrong door. They wouldn't grab the folder from my hands by force—would they? These were *my* instructions. I'd demand that they phone the Department of Instructions, Major Erms ... But then, they would know all that, so why should I worry myself to death? Quickly I tried to review the whole chain of events, to prepare my report according to procedure. I couldn't contradict myself; that would be fatal. But I was so confused. For example, did that whole affair with the little old man take place before or after they arrested my first guide in the hall? I took a deep breath and turned the doorknob.

There wasn't a soul in the large, gloomy office, only cabinets and catalogs of all sizes and descriptions, huge ledgers, piles of papers tied with string, jars of glue, scissors, blotters, rubber stamps and all sorts of office debris all over the big desks along the walls. I heard feet shuffling; in a doorway off to the side there appeared an old, disheveled man in a uniform full of ink spots.

"You came to see us?" he croaked. "A rare guest indeed! Welcome, welcome! What can we do for you? Something to be checked out, no doubt?"

But before I could say a word, the old man rattled on, vigorously sniffing as he talked, trying to sniff back the disgusting drop that hung at the tip of his nose.

"Civilian clothes, you're in civilian clothes, that means you want something from the catalog . . . just a minute, it's all right here . . ."

He hobbled over to a huge card file and began to pull out one drawer after another. I looked around the room again. There were piles of junk all over the floor, in the corners, under the chairs; the air was thick with dust and the smell of molding paper. The old geezer rasped in explanation:

"Chief Archive Custodian Glouble ain't here. He's at a meeting, don't you know. The Underclerk ain't here either, he didn't give a reason, he just left. So you see, sir, here I am all by my lonesome to watch the store. It's Antheus Kappril at your service, sir, Custodian Ninth Degree, ready for retirement after forty-eight years of faithful service, believe it or not. Oh yes, it's the life of leisure for me all right, that's what they tell me! But on the other hand, sir, as you can see for yourself, I'm indispensable here! Indispensable! But here I am talking away and you're in a frightful hurry, I bet. Business, business. You place your call slips in this little old box here and lean on the buzzer when you're ready; I come in a jiffy, find what you need even quicker, and if you want to read it here, no problem, and if you don't, then put your serial number here, under the fifth column, IV-B, and that's all there is to it."

He concluded this gravelly monologue with an odd little dance intended as a bow—or else his legs were giving way —and he pointed invitingly at the card file, gave an ingratiating smile, then began to back away.

"Kappril," I suddenly asked, afraid to look him in the eye, "is—is the Department of Investigation on this floor?"

"Come again?" He cupped his ear with his hand. "Department of what? Didn't hear you, didn't hear you."

"Or the Prosecution Bureau?" I went on, ignoring the possible consequences of such open inquiry.

"Prosecution Bureau?..." He seemed genuinely perplexed. "Never heard of it, sir, we're the only department here, I never heard of that other..."

"These are the Archives?"

"That's us. The Archives, Records, the Library... Anything else we can do for you?"

"Not right now, thank you."

"No need to thank me, it's my job, it's my job. Here's the buzzer, don't forget to buzz."

He shuffled out, then I heard a fit of violent coughing from the next room. Or was someone trying to strangle him? But the sound faded, and I was alone with endless rows of drawers, their labels framed in brass.

What did this mean? Were they trying to learn my interests? What could they possibly gain from that? My eyes wandered over the labels. The catalog was arranged by subject, not alphabetically— ESCHATOSCOPY, THEOLOGY, PONTIFICES AND ARTIFICES, APPLIED CADAVEROLOGY. I tried THEOLOGY. The cards were in no apparent order:

ANGELS—*see* Communicants, Communiqués. Air power. *Also see* Daily orders (Give us this day our—).

LOVE—*see* Diversion. *Also see* Treason (But hate the traitor).

RESURRECTION—*see* Cadaverology. Corpse Corps.

COMMUNION WITH THE SAINTS—*see* Contact.

What could I lose? I filled out a call slip for one of the daily orders under ANGELS. But then there were so many headings which made little or no sense: INFERNALISTICS, SCUTTLENAUTICS, DECEREBRATION, BODY-AND-SOULGUARDS, RETROCARNATION. I couldn't bother with them all; the card file was much too big, its wooden pillars reached the ceiling. Even the most superficial survey would take weeks, months. By now I had removed quite a pile of green, pink and white cards from the drawers; some had fallen to the floor. I started to put them back, one at a time. It seemed to take forever. With a glance over my shoulder to see if anyone was watching, I began to stuff the cards in any which way.

Could it be that the catalog was in such disorder precisely because others had wandered in here, just as I did? On one desk nearby stood a row of bulky black volumes, apparently an encyclopedia of some kind. I opened the volume marked *S* to look up SCUTTLENAUTICS. "SCRAMBLED EGGS—the best breakfast against interception." No, that wasn't it. "SCUTTLENAUTICS—the science of nonnavigation. *See also* Abortive Sailing, Mock Docking." I tried volume *A*. Under AGENT (SUB, SUPER, PROVOCATEUR) was a long paragraph and underneath that, an article entitled "AGENTS AND THEIR AGENCIES FROM EARLIEST TIMES TO THE PRESENT DAY."

Another volume lay open on the desk, and I read: "ORIGINAL SIN—the division of the world into Information and Misinformation." I skipped from page to page, volume to volume, reading wherever my eye fell on an interesting definition. "RETROCARNATION—1) a Red that goes back on his word; 2) disembodiment, dematerialization—*see* THIN AIR, POWDER, LAMB." Then there was a whole list of odd items under DECEREBRATION: persuasion by quartering, screws for screws, breaking codes without bones, fundamental flaying, and so forth. But I was tired of leafing through these dusty tomes; I wanted to see Major Erms. Yes, Erms would help me, I'd tell him everything! Suddenly there was a shuffling—the old man had returned. He eyed me sharply from the doorway, smiled and raised his spectacles to the top of his bald head. It was only now that I noticed he was cross-eyed. That is, one eye watched me while the other wandered up, as if seeking inspiration from above.

"Find what you wanted?"

He squinted, whistled under his breath. (A signal?)

Then he saw a card on the floor, one I'd missed, looked at it and said:

"Ah . . . that too?" He clucked appreciatively as he picked it up with grimy fingers. "In that case, won't you come this way, sir? It's hard for an old codger like me to carry out such heavy volumes. Of course, they're not all heavy, but . . . you've been cleared, haven't you? You look like one of General Mlassgrack's men, you do. Professional secrecy, confidential, top security, don't I know, heh-heh! Follow me, follow me, watch yourself, don't get dirty . . . the dust, you know!"

Rambling on in this way, he led me down a narrow, winding passage into the stacks. I kept bumping into atlases and folios as we went deeper into that murky labyrinth.

"Here!" my guide exclaimed at last in triumph. A bright, naked bulb lit up a fairly roomy alcove. We were surrounded by shelves that sagged beneath the weight of gray, crumbling books.

"Cake!" he snorted, waving the card in front of my nose. That was indeed the word on the card. "Cake, sir, help yourself to a slice . . . heh-heh! It's all here—there's your Splanchnology, Innardry, Disemboweling and Reembowelment, Viscerators and Eviscerators. An original edition over here, *De crucificatione modo primario divino,* second-century, the only copy in existence, wonderfully preserved, and with illustrations. Look at those shackles, will you, and here's flaying alive, there's playing dead, hamstringing, stringing up, tests of personal endurance . . . Now, on the next shelf—no, that's Physical Tortures. I'm sorry, we're in this section here—Bruises on the left, and on the right, Juices."

"Juices?" I couldn't help asking.

"Juices, juices. For example, a spit, an open fire, and you have juices, don't you? Yes, and on the next shelf—Empaling. Mahagony, birch, oak, ash. And Bruises, they're easy—but you must know all about it! Ah, nobody ever drops in any more, one gets so lonely . . . It's so nice to

have a little company, sir, if you know what I mean . . .
They say this is all old-fashioned, obsolete."

"Obsolete?"

"Oh, yes. Leave it to the butchers, they say. Top secret
sirloin, tenderized—Lieutenant Pirpitschek likes to joke.
But things are picking up again, it seems, in our department . . . The dust here, the dust is just awful!"

He beat the dust off his sleeves and went on:

"Allusions to cake, revolutions for cake—let them eat
cake, wasn't it? Ninety entries, all in all, a regular bakery,
like our General says—oh, there's a real man, the head of
something terribly important, don't you know! 'Custodian
Kappril, at your service, sir!' I say. But he, does he give me
the book number right off? Not on your life! He hums a
little tune—hum hum, hum hum—and I know exactly what
he wants. Every time! . . . Dr. Mrayznorl is in charge here
—what's this? *De strangulatione systematica occulta.* Somebody must have put it here by mistake, that's physical—
and Mummification too, tsk-tsk. Excuse me, that's Crypt-
analysis over there, you don't want that—or do you? Take
a look if you like, by all means . . . We have some very interesting books. That one you're holding, allow me, I'll
wipe it off for you—it's wipe off or be wiped out, like our
General says. Heh-heh! He's wonderful with words, oh
yes . . . What's that you're holding—ah, *The Universe in
a Drawer*—what's his name again? Hyde, yes. A bit old-
fashioned, but not bad. The Subcustodian of Archives
spoke highly of it, and he's an expert in the field. *Life in a
Lavatory?* Why would you want *that?*"

I put the book back hastily and pulled out another. My
head was beginning to spin; an unbearable smell, over-
whelming but unidentifiable, perhaps a little like mildew,
or even sandpaper—this heavy, nauseating breath of the
moldering centuries seemed to pervade everything.

I should have settled for anything, taken the first book
that came to hand and left. But I kept browsing, as if I
were really looking for something. It certainly wasn't *The*

Deontology of Treason, nor the small, dog-eared *In Imitation of Nothing,* nor the black handbook *Updating the Transcendental,* which for some reason was shelved in the Espionage section. Around a corner was a row of thick tomes, their bindings brittle with age and the paper spotted and yellow. The illustrations were woodcuts, as was the frontispiece of *The Compleat Spye, or, Everyman's Handbooke of Espyonage yn Three Partes, Prolegomena & Paralipomena by the Author-Nugator Jonahberry O. Paupus.* Between these bulky works were several incunabula, their covers torn and barely legible: *Cloak-and-Dagger without Guesswork, Anarchy by Remote Control, The Bribe—a Spy's Best Friend, Snooping in Theory and Practice.* There was a bibliography of scopological and scopognostic literature, including scoposcopy. *Machina Speculatrix, or, The Tactics of Counterespionage. Cohabitation and Collaboration. The Fine Art of Treachery* and *The Constant Traitor. Do-it-yourself Denunciation. Favorite Blunders and Slipups* with full diagrams. *Traps and Taps.* There were even artistic items—a musical score with the title carefully written in violet, *The Walls Have Ears, a Divertimento for Four Trombones and Hidden Mike,* and a collection of sonnets entitled *Microdots.*

Someone groaned. It was a terrible, heartrending groan that came from behind a partition. I grabbed the old man's sleeve and asked:

"What was that?"

"Ah yes, the recruits are listening to records. It's a seminar on Applied Agony, Simulthanasia, or something like that. Tombsters, we call them," he muttered.

And indeed, that same groan was being played over and over again. I was ready to leave. But the old geezer fell into a fever of activity; he bustled about the shelves, jumped up on tiptoe, moved the rusty ladders here and there, darted up the rungs, threw books down, and in general raised a thick cloud of dust—all this to regale me with yet another exhibit, some decrepit rarity or other. And he never ceased his ranting and raving, almost to the rhythm of the howling behind the partition. The glistening drop at the tip of his nose swung wildly but never fell. Somehow, his cross-eyed gaze never left me, so I had to be very careful—he might discover I was here under false pretenses, an impostor. But no, he continued his frantic inspection, eager to show me still another dusty volume. *Basic Cryptology* was pressed into my hands and fell open to these words: "The human body consists of the following places of concealment. . ."

"Ah, here is *Homo Sapiens As a Corpus Delicti,* a splendid work, splendid . . . and this is *Incendiaries Then and Now,* and here's a list of the experts in the field—listen: Meern, Birdhoove, Fishmi, Cantovo, Karck, and we're in it too of course, there's our Professor Barbeliese, Klauderlaut, Grumpf—imagine that, Grumpf! This? *The Morbitron* by Glauble. Yes, he's an author as well . . . heh-heh! Now this pamphlet—"

He pulled out a stack of disintegrating cards.

"Umbilicomurology and, yes, the breeding and care of coypus—there isn't anything we don't have here . . . What you're holding there, that's Fashion. You know, the cut of the straitjacket, things like that . . . Here are some other items: *The ABC's of Self-surveillance, Automated Self-immolation . . .*"

I backed away, trying to defend myself against this flood of talk and dust and decay, this barrage of strange terminology—triple tails, coded leaks, spotted caches, exposed plants, strategic lays, integrated risks, sensitive channels, high-grade rendezvous entrapment . . .

Unable to take any more, I told the old man I had to leave. He glanced at his watch, a large silver onion.

"Is that a secret watch?" I asked.

"Of course it's a secret watch, what do you think?"

He put it back in his pocket and frowned as I mumbled some excuse about dropping in another time to pick out what I needed . . . He didn't seem to hear, he kept wanting

79

to take me to other sections. Naked bulbs lit up the crowded shelves and cabinets like low-hung stars. Even at the exit he tried to show me another book, pointing out special pages, praising the work as if I were a potential buyer and he a half-mad bibliopole or bibliophile.

"But you took nothing, sir! You took nothing!" he pestered me all the way back to the catalog room. To get rid of him, I asked for the book on angels and a handbook of astronomy. I signed for them illegibly and left, a thick manuscript under my arm—the book on angels, as it turned out, had never been published. I took a deep breath of fresh air out in the corridor. What a relief! But my clothes still carried the smell of rotting leather, bookbinder's glue and parchment. I felt like I'd just stepped out of a slaughterhouse.

6

I had hardly left the Archives when a thought hit me. I returned and compared the door number with the one scribbled on my card: sure enough, I had made a mistake, I had taken the second digit for an eight instead of a three. So my real destination was 3383.

The fact that I had made a mistake and misread a number was a tremendous comfort to me. Until now, everything had seemed accidental but in reality had gone according to some plan. But this visit to the Archives, that was a genuine accident. And the Building was responsible for it: the room number had been written in too carelessly. Human error, then, still operated here; mystery and freedom were still in the realm of possibility.

Then too, the examining magistrate was as much to blame as I, the defendant—we would have a good laugh together and the matter would be dismissed. I headed for 3383 confidently.

Judging from the great number of phones on every desk, 3383 was not just another office. I went straight to the head official's door—but found no knob to turn. The receptionist asked if she could be of any help. My explanation grew involved and complicated because I couldn't tell her the truth.

"But you have no appointment," she repeated over and over again. I demanded an appointment. But that was out of the question, she said; I would have to submit my petition in triplicate through the proper channels, then get the necessary signatures. But my Mission was Special, Top Secret. I tried to explain without raising my voice; it could only be discussed in absolute privacy. But she was busy with the phones—answering with a word or two here, pressing a button or two there, putting some people on hold, cutting off others—and hardly seemed to be aware of my existence.

After an hour of this I swallowed my pride and began to plead with her. But pleading didn't have the least effect, so I showed her the contents of my folder, the blueprint of the Building, the outline for Operation Shovel. I might have been showing her old newspapers for all the response this produced. She was the perfect secretary: nothing existed beyond the narrow limits of her routine. Driven to desperate measures, I let out a stream of terrible confessions—I told her about the open safe, about how I had unwittingly caused the suicide of the little old man, and as none of this made the least impression on her, I began to invent things, I confessed to treason, high treason, anything, if only she would let me in. I demanded the worst—arrest, dishonor—I screamed in her ear. But she waved me away as if I were a fly, and continued to answer the phones with complete indifference. Finally, bathed in sweat, weak and trembling, I collapsed into a chair in the corner. Very well, I would wait. The examining magistrate, the prosecutor, whoever was hiding behind that office door had to come out sooner or later. To pass the time, I leafed through the manuscript I had with me. But I was too confused and wrought-up to concentrate. It said something about the sighting of angels. The astronomy handbook wasn't any easier to follow—there were long paragraphs on galactic camouflage, nebulae prototypes, relocation of planets, cosmic sabotage . . . I read the same page ten times without understanding a thing. The hours passed. Surely, this nightmare was worse than any torture I could have ever imagined. Countless times I got up to ask the receptionist questions in a feeble voice. Could she please tell me what time it was? When did her boss go out for lunch? Were there any other investigative offices or prosecution departments nearby? She advised me to try Information. And where was Information, I asked. Room 1593, she said and picked up another phone. So I gathered up my papers, the folder and the book, and walked out, totally crushed. There was nothing left of my earlier confidence, the calm I had achieved that morning, absolutely nothing. My watch informed me that I had spent practically an entire day in that office. Or an entire night, since time was relative in the Building.

There was no room 1593. It would have had to have been on the first level, and the last door at the very end of the corridor was 1591. I tried several different rooms, wherever there was a "Secret," "Top Secret," or "Headquarters." I even looked for the office of my Commander in Chief. Nothing. Perhaps they'd changed the signs or the numbers. The papers were growing limp in my sweaty hands. I hadn't had a thing to eat since yesterday and was faint with hunger. My face itched, I needed a shave. After considerable wandering around, I took to questioning the elevator men. The one with the artificial leg told me room 1591 wasn't "on the list." You had to call first. After another four hours (twice I managed to use a phone in some empty room, but Information was busy), the traffic in the halls increased, everyone was heading for the cafeteria. I joined the crowd. Today it was macaroni and cheese—terrible, but it put off the moment when I would have to set forth again. I thought about Major Erms—if he failed me, I had nothing left. Odd, how my confessions and self-accusations hadn't been accepted. But I wasn't surprised. Nothing seemed to surprise me any more. My hands covered with grease and my face in a cold sweat, I returned to my bathroom, folded a towel for a pillow and lay down by the tub. Almost instantly I was seized with a nameless, irrational fear, a fear so powerful that I began to shiver on the tiled floor. It was no use—I got up, aching all over, sat on the rim of the tub and tried to think through what had happened and guess what lay in store. The folder, the book, the manuscript on angels lay at my feet. I tried to think, but couldn't. I paced the bathroom floor, turned the faucets on and watched the water, turned them off slowly to see exactly at what point the whining in the pipes started, then I made faces at myself in the mirror, I even cried a little, then sat on the rim of the tub again, my head in my hands. Hours passed. Was this all still a test? Could my misreading of the room number have been foreseen, even intentionally arranged? The old librarian had led me to the section on physical torture . . . Wait a minute, torture—torture—torte! Torte was a kind of cake, wasn't it? Yes, a kind of cake . . . Ah, how devious they were! Did they mean to tell me that—that I would be tortured? The torture of waiting. Then there *was* a plan here, a plan to push me to the limit, to test my fiber, my endurance for the Mission, that "highly dangerous" Mission. Then I was still in favor, still singled out? In that case, everything would be all right; I had only to maintain an air of indifference, passivity. Yes, the receptionist had deliberately ignored me, and Information had been inaccessible by design. Comforted by that thought, I washed my face and went out to find Major Erms. Outside the Department of Instructions I saw an unusually large number of janitors polishing the floor. They wore brand-new overalls and didn't seem to pay too much attention to their work. They were looking around instead. All were squat, solidly built, with broad shoulders; all wore caps a size too small. They could have passed for brothers. Each one nudged the next and muttered something.

Several officers came up in full dress, sabers at their side. They asked to see the janitors' papers, the janitors asked to see their papers. Somehow I was overlooked. Obviously a security precaution—something was up! I waited around, curious. Also, I was in no particular hurry to see Major Erms. Then, suddenly, a bugle blared, everyone rushed to stand in place, they lined up at attention, the elevator opened, two adjutants in silver braid stood guard.

"The Admiral! The Admiral!" the news went around. The officers and janitors fell into formation and saluted. My heart pounded with excitement; now I would get to see a high-ranking dignitary. From an elevator that had the most elegant interior (the walls were in cut velvet and decorated with maps, portraits and heraldry), a little old man stepped out, his uniform blazing with gold. He was short and gray, had liver spots and limped a little. He surveyed his men and without the least effort (you could see he was a professional) bellowed:

"At ease!"

The Admiral walked up and down the column of men, dissatisfied, suspicious—and stopped in front of me. Then I realized I was the only civilian there. My first impulse was to fall at his feet, confess everything, beg for mercy— but I stood there instead, looking as loyal as I possibly could. He eyed me fiercely, like a warrior, jangled his medals, then barked:

"Civilian?"

"Yes, sir! Civilian, sir!"

"In the Service?"

"Yes, sir! In the Ser—"

"Wife? Children?"

"Beg to report, sir—"

"H'm," he said with a paternal smile. He mulled something over, frowned, absently fingered the plump wart under his nose. I watched his liver spots and waited.

"An undercover man," he said in a hoarse whisper. "An undercover man, good. Follow me."

My heart in my mouth, I stepped out of the column and followed the Admiral, painfully aware of the whispering behind my back. We marched down the corridor, and at each department we passed, officers jumped out and saluted. There was the Department of Promotion and Demotion, the Exhumation and Fumigation Hall, the Debilitation and Rehabilitation Section. The last door was marked "Degrading." Here the Admiral stopped, and the chief of that department leaped out and snapped to attention.

"H'm?" asked the Admiral in a confidential tone.

"Counterdecoration, sir."

85

And he whispered the exact proceedings of the ceremony. All I caught was: "... off ... humiliation ... without ... drummed out ... awful ..."

"H'm!" said the Admiral. Sternly, he adjusted his medals and stepped across the threshold of the Degrading Department, stopped, turned to me and snapped, "You! Undercover man! Follow me!"

The room was huge, splendid in a funereal way—luxurious black drapes, heavy antique mirrors suspended from the ceiling and increasing the gloom with their cloudy surfaces, and in the corners large pieces of furniture resembling catafalques. In the middle of the room, surrounded by these lifeless spectators of the forthcoming counterdecoration ceremony, five officers stood at attention on a magnificent carpet featuring snakes and Judases; they were in full regalia—aiguillettes and epaulettes, insignia and crests, sabers at their sides. Deathly pale, they stiffened at the Admiral's entrance—their medals sparkled, their tassels trembled—that was the only sign of life. The Admiral looked them over carefully, then stopped in front of one officer and hurled the word:

"Disgrace!"

He paused, as if something wasn't quite right, and gave me a sign to switch off the overhead lights. The room was now fairly dark; the mirrors had a ghostly aspect to them. But still the Admiral wasn't satisfied. He stepped back until the dim light caught the silver in his hair. Then he took a deep breath.

"Disgrace!!" he roared in their faces. "Disgrace!!!" Then he paused, uncertain whether the first "Disgrace" should count or not. Just then, a halo of light played about his medals—a good effect—so he decided to continue. "Stain! On your honor! Blot! On your record! Shame! Traitors! Turncoats!"

Now he was warming up, getting the feel of it. "Never!" he thundered, this time with more dignity. "I will not permit! You dared! From this time on! I'll break you!!"

That, I thought, would be the end of it. But no, he was

only just beginning. He went up to the first officer, stood on his toes and tore at one of the jeweled medals that decorated the officer's chest. It came off like a ripe pear. Now there was no turning back. He began ripping everything off, ripping wildly, with complete abandon, like someone tearing the possessions off a corpse on a battlefield—aiguillettes, crests, tassels, whatever he could reach and grab. Then to the second officer, like a beast of prey, ripping and tearing—the seams came apart easily. They must have tailors to do that specially, I thought. Honors, decorations, medals rained and flashed on the carpet. The Admiral ground them under his heel. The five officers stood passively under this onslaught, their pale faces reflected and multiplied in the dim mirrors—as were their torn insignia and shredded uniforms. The old man walked up and down this avenue of shame, then leaned against me for a moment to catch his breath, then returned—to slap the men in the face. Then, their swords: he pulled them from their scabbards, one by one, and handed them to me to break across my knee. The fact that I was a civilian made the humiliation that much greater, of course. The ceremony over, we left the darkened Degrading Department, passed through Decoration Hall, also full of suspended mirrors, and came to a highly ornate door. An aide opened it for us.

The Admiral and I were alone in an enormous office. There was a desk of gigantic proportions, and behind that, a deep armchair. On the walls were imposing portraits of the Admiral, wise and full of authority. In a corner stood a statue of the Admiral on horseback. The live Admiral took off his hat, loosened his collar and gave a sigh of relief. He even loosened his belt a notch and winked. Clearly, I was being taken into his confidence. Should I answer with a smile? No, he might think that impudent. The old man sank into his armchair and breathed heavily. Why didn't he take off all those medals? They must have been a tremendous weight to carry around. He seemed to age right before my eyes.

"An undercover man," he muttered to himself, "an undercover man." Apparently this amused him. Or was he, for all his great power and authority, turning a little senile? Then again, compelled as he was to live in uniform all his life, perhaps he nurtured some secret fondness for civilian things. They would be forbidden fruit for him.

"An undercover man. An undercover man? . . ."

He grunted affirmatively, clicked his tongue, cracked his knuckles—all this in the most casual way—but there was a purpose behind it, I knew. He looked me over and coughed politely. What, didn't he trust me?

Why did he look at my legs? An allusion to my earlier impulse to fall on my knees before him and confess?

"Undercover man!" he wheezed. I sprang to my feet. He flinched and raised his hands.

"Not too close! Stay where you are! Sing me a song, undercover man, sing me a song!" he shouted. I understood: afraid of treachery, the experienced old man was having me sing so that I could hide nothing from him.

I sang whatever came into my head. He pointed to a side drawer and nodded for me to pull it out, which I did as I sang. The drawer was filled with little jars and smelled like an old-fashioned pharmacy. He gestured for me to take the jars out and line them up on his desk, which I did as I sang. He watched me anxiously, then sat up in his armchair, lifted the sleeve of his jacket, and with great caution peeled off his white glove. The hand was withered, spotty, full of veins; it had something on it that looked like a bug. In an urgent whisper, he ordered me to stop singing and hand him a pill from a gold jar. This he swallowed with extreme difficulty. Finally, when the pill was got down, he had me bring him a pitcher of water, pour some into a glass and measure in a liquid medicine.

"Careful, undercover man!" he whispered nervously. "That stuff's strong—don't spill it!"

"Of course not, Admiral sir! Never!" I cried, touched by his trust in me. The trembling of his spotted, mole-covered hand became more pronounced as I began to add the medicine to his glass with an eyedropper.

"One, two, three, four," he counted the drops. At sixteen he screeched: "Stop!" I jumped, but fortunately the next drop stayed at the end of the dropper and didn't fall in. Why sixteen? Apprehensive, I gave him the glass.

Good . . . good, undercover man," he said, no less apprehensive. "You . . . if you don't mind . . . you . . . you try it first, yes?"

I drank a little. It took him several minutes to drink the rest himself. His teeth kept chattering against the glass—he had to remove them. They made a broken white bracelet there on the desk. At last, with a martyred look, he managed to down the liquid. I held his hand to steady it—it felt like small bones loose inside a leather bag. If only he wouldn't faint on me.

"Admiral, sir . . ." I said, "would you allow me to present my case?"

He closed his clouded eyes and seemed to shrink behind the desk as he listened to my feverish words. While I talked, he put his hand out—evidently he wished me to remove the other glove. Then he rested this hand on the one with the bug and coughed, listening intently to the rattle in his chest. But I continued to unfold before him my tangled tale of woe. Surely his infirmities would make him sympathetic toward the frailties of others; he would understand. His face, all covered with liver spots and moles, grew smaller between the misshapen ears, assumed more and more that look of patriarchal deterioration that so inspired my filial pity and respect. There were all sorts of growths—one, on the top of his balding head, looked like a downy egg. But were these not the scars of wounds sustained in the battle with implacable time, and did they not give him an air of the utmost venerability?

Wishing my confession to appear as sincere as possible, I sat at his elbow and told him the whole, sad story of my mistakes, my slip-ups and defeats. I didn't leave out a thing. His measured breathing, his nodding, the occasional smile that played over his open lips—all this comforted me, encouraged me, made me feel he was on my side. As I came

89

to the end of my story, I leaned over and touched his arm —even that departure from regulations seemed to meet with his indulgence. Now filled with the highest hopes and at the same time deeply moved by my own words, I finally made my impassioned plea:

"Will you help me, Admiral sir? Tell me what to do!"

Of course, he needed time to reflect on all that I had said. But after an hour or two I thought it prudent to repeat, in the way of a reminder:

"What should I do, sir?"

He continued to nod, as if encouraging me to go on. But his face was turned away. Could it be that he was ashamed of the part he had played in the Building's plot against me?

Holding my breath, I moved even closer—and saw that he was asleep. He had been sleeping the whole time. The medicine must have helped. Now that I was silent, his sleep became deeper, he began to dream. There was a clicking in his throat, suddenly a whistle, then some cautious hissing, another whistle, a more determined whistle, a bold blast on the horn, a call to the hunt, and then I could hear all the sounds of the hunt, the rustling trees, the shouts, the galloping through dale and glen, an occasional shot carried by the wind, muffled and distant . . . then silence, then again the horn, and the chase renewed . . . I got up and tried to brush the bug off his hand. It wasn't a bug at all.

I took a closer look: dark spots, growths, myriads of moles, some flat and dry, some like the comb of a rooster, others sprouting hair with unseemly impudence . . .

His uniform, I knew, was his refuge, his support, the thing that kept him in one piece, held him together—what a risk he had taken to unbutton and loosen it like that— I didn't realize how great a risk until I saw him now at close quarters! No wonder he insisted on my keeping at a distance! At a distance there was only an innocent snoring, an ordinary flapping in the throat; close up, there was a veritable jungle of growths, wild, abandoned growths, growths that burrowed and spread in stealth. What madness of the skin was this? A dermatological fantasy in the manner of the Baroque? A self-willed, autonomous creation above hardening arteries? No, rather a rebellion, an uprising in the provinces, on the periphery of the organism! An attempt to break away, to escape in all directions! The hairy warts, the moles, the growths all grew, preparing themselves in secret, readying themselves to flee the worn-out biological matrix—as if by this dispersion they could avoid the inevitable end.

A fine situation! Here was the Admiral—and here were these unsolicited pranks of nature, fully intending by their secret proliferation to survive him, survive him in the form of common warts!

This changed things. Obviously, the old man was in no condition to help me. However, if he was unable to show me the way, to give me a sign, then perhaps . . . perhaps he was the sign himself, perhaps a message was being sent *through him*.

An interesting thought. I took another close look at the Admiral: no doubt about it, these bumps and nodules, these neoplasms and lesions went far beyond the bounds of decency; the old man was being used, manipulated, made to sprout and multiply, grow spots and stains and hooves and bugs—see how that meaty birthmark beneath his eye flushed pink like the dawn of a new day! Shameful! Disgraceful!

No, these arrogant claims, boasts to have discovered new forms, new means of creative expression, they led to the dead end of plagiarism. There was a cauliflower, for example, and here was plainly a mushroom, and here an obvious borrowing from poultry.

If that were only all! But this amounted to desertion, treason! A generation of aggressive, hardy dwarfs feeding on a dying man's sweat! I had before me—was nothing sacred?!—a cruel mockery, a jeering at the dignity of the soon-to-be-deceased.

There was no longer any doubt. Here was no subtle hint,

but a clear answer, a brutal rejection of all my lame explanations, excuses and arguments.

I sat down, shattered. It was immaterial now whether that answer came from him or through him. In either case it was the Building that spoke. What fantastic cunning, to utilize even the approach of death, the very marks of its proximity, to conduct official business!

Still, this was no final solution. They were merely letting me know that everything had been taken note of, all my little sins, impersonations, excuses, treasons. I was being given a reprieve; the time for sentencing had not yet come.

Cut the Gordian knot or be strangled by it, be convicted or found pure as the driven snow . . . as if my destiny was to have some monument raised in my name—either in this Building or the *other!* Any moment now guards could break in and seize me, arrest me, terminate me. But such tactics were out of fashion. Besides, they knew I couldn't stay here by the sleeping Admiral now that I had received the message, they knew I would take up my wandering again, like a dog nursing its injured paw.

Suddenly angry, I paced the luxurious carpet. The Admiral sat in his armchair, shrunken, so unlike the hale and hearty portraits that stared out fiercely from the walls. I looked around with the impatience of a thief, feeling that as yet I had done nothing of consequence, that even my transgressions hardly counted for anything. If only I could attract attention to myself, do something spectacular, rise or fall, it didn't matter . . . even disaster would be a victory . . . even the worst crime . . .

The desk had an unusual number of locks; it evidently contained valuable documents. I knelt and pulled gently at one of the drawers. Inside were cardboard boxes tied with rubber bands and marked "one teaspoon three times a day," and there was a strongbox full of pills. The next drawer had more of the same: nothing but medicine. I found a bunch of keys and proceeded to try them, one by one, in the locks, getting down on all fours behind the desk. No, this they hadn't foreseen, that I would be capable of such a low deed, rifling the Admiral's desk, and under his very nose! There was no turning back now; this was not the sort of thing one could explain away later. My hands trembled as I pulled out box after box, tore the wrappings off packages —nothing, nothing but bottles, vials, jars of salve, tranquilizers, Band-Aids, medicine for corns, suppositories, supports and trusses, safety pins, cotton balls and cotton swabs, all sorts of sprays and powders, eyedroppers, tweezers, thermometers. That was all?!

Impossible! It was a trick! Camouflage! I tapped the remaining drawers. I felt around, heard the click of a hidden spring, reached in and pulled out—a cap, a stick, a slingshot, a spotted stone, a dried leaf, and—aha!—a sealed packet. I broke the seal and several cards fell out, the kind that come with bubble gum. What else? Nothing else.

They were animal cards: a donkey, a zebra, a buffalo, a baboon, a hyena, and an egg. A donkey? That meant . . . I was an ass? What about an elephant? Awkward, thick-skinned. Hyena? Let's see, a hyena fed on carrion . . . the old man? And a baboon? Baboon, monkey, monkey business, ape—an ape apes, of course! Then . . . they had anticipated my attempted burglary . . . and the egg? What did the egg say?

I turned the card over. Ah! The cuckoo. The cuckoo puts her egg in another bird's nest—an act of treachery, falsification! What then? Assault? Murder? But how could I murder that poor old man with moles? Anyway . . .

"Peep," he mumbled under his breath and began to snore in a tremolo, like a nightingale, a very old nightingale.

That was the last straw. I threw everything back in the drawers, brushed off my knees, stepped over a puddle of spilled medicine, and collapsed into a chair. Not to deliberate on what I should do next, but just to collapse—to collapse in despair and exhaustion.

7

I have no idea how long I sat there. The old man gave an occasional snort in his sleep, but that couldn't rouse me from my stupor. Several times I got up and went to see Major Erms, and it always turned out to be a dream. Then the thought occurred to me that I could simply sit there, just sit there—they'd have to do something about it eventually. Except what about those long, long hours I had spent in that horrible reception room? No, they'd let me rot first . . .

Quickly, I gathered up my papers and went to Major Erms. He was at his desk, writing something with one hand and stirring coffee with the other. He lifted his blue eyes and looked straight at me. There was a cheerful strength in those eyes, the joyful attitude of a puppy pleased with everything, a puppy . . . a dog . . . was there something in that? But he interrupted my thoughts by saying:

"You're late! I was beginning to think—poof!—into thin air! Where were you?"

"With the Admiral," I said, taking a seat. He tilted his head in a gesture of mock respect.

"Indeed," he said. "You don't waste time. I should have known."

"Cut that out!" I yelled, rising from my chair, my fists clenched.

"What?" he gasped, astonished. But I didn't let him speak. The dam had burst and my words came pouring out and nothing could stop them—I told him about my first meanderings through the Building, about the Commander in Chief, about the suspicion which even then had taken hold of me like an illness, and I told him how that suspicion had affected all my subsequent actions, how I was ready to accept the role of martyr, an innocent man convicted on circumstantial evidence, a man without a single blot on his record, and how I had prepared myself for the worst, but even the worst had been denied me and I was left to myself, always to myself, always infernally alone, and I told him how I wandered from door to door on business that made no sense, no sense to anyone . . . I told him everything, but even as I told him, I knew it was in vain. I repeated myself, I groped for words, circled, feeling something was missing, something didn't quite hold together . . . Then a thought hit me, and I began to think out loud, think the whole thing out—that is, if I were to be of any use at all (putting aside all personal claims, illusions, hopes), then wasn't it foolish, even criminal, to waste me in this way? What would the Building gain if I fell to pieces? Nothing! Then what purpose did all this nonsense serve, and wasn't it about time they called it quits and gave me back my instructions, acquainted me with at least the general idea of the Mission, whatever that might be? For my part, I could guarantee that I would endeavor, with all my heart and soul, above and beyond the call of duty, pledging loyalty, faith, devotion . . .

Unfortunately my speech, chaotic enough to begin with, did not improve towards the end. Out of breath, shaken, I stopped in mid-sentence. Major Erms's blue eyes stared at me in consternation. Then he lowered them and stirred his coffee, fumbling with the spoon—ah, he was embarrassed, embarrassed for me!

"Really, I don't know . . ." he began in a quiet and friendly way, though I thought I detected a note of severity in his voice. "I don't know what to do with you. To take such risks . . . such schoolboy pranks . . . opening medicine chests, really! It's painful even to mention it! How could you let your imagination run away with you like that?" He was increasingly stern, yet somehow still maintained that incredibly sunny disposition of his.

This time however I was not going to be led around by the nose. I said quickly:

"And my instructions? Why didn't you explain them to me? Prandtl categorically refused to. In fact, he actually —he stole them from me—"

"He *what?*"

"He didn't do it himself, there was this fat officer in the room ... but Prandtl knew about it, I'm positive."

"Oh, so you're positive. That's nice. And do you have any proof of this?"

"No," I admitted—but immediately resumed the offensive: "Look, Major Erms, if you really want to help me, tell me right now what was in those instructions!"

And I looked him in the eye.

"So that's what you're after!" He burst out laughing. "My dear fellow, how could I possibly remember? Really, there are so many—just look!" He picked up thick stacks of paper from the desk and waved them in the air. "You honestly expect me to remember all this? Come on, have a heart ..."

"No!" I said firmly. "I don't believe you! You say you don't remember anything? Not even the general idea? Well, I just don't believe you!!"

If only I hadn't gone too far. After all, he was the only man I could count on, my last resort. Even now, I felt this. If he were suddenly to confess that he was only acting under orders, that he was not what he seemed to be, not Major Erms the honest young man with friendly, blue eyes but just another part of the Building—then nothing remained for me but to go to that bathroom upstairs and ...

Major Erms did not speak for a long while. He rubbed his forehead, he scratched his ear, he sighed.

"You lost your instructions," he finally said. "All right. That's *something*. It calls for disciplinary action. I'll have to initiate proceedings. But don't worry, it won't be bad— unless you left the premises at any time. You didn't leave the Building, I hope?"

"No."

"Thank God!" he sighed with relief. "In that case, the

whole thing will be a mere formality. We'll take care of it later. As far as what you've said in this office is concerned, I didn't hear any of it, understand? If I listened every time a colleague blew off steam here, well—I wouldn't be fit to hold this position!" His fist hit the desk. "You doubt my sincerity. Why should I like you, you wonder, when we hardly know each other?" He spread his arms. "But it isn't like that at all. Please pay attention to what I have to say. I'm not just another petty official pouring over a lot of meaningless papers, I'm not another blasted bureaucrat! I'm a terminal, a port, a stopping-off point for our very best people, people who are on their way—*there*. Now, you've been singled out for a Special Mission. So while I don't know you personally, I do know that on that basis alone (not everyone gets a Mission, after all) you merit my respect, my trust, my friendship—particularly as your work demands that you will be alone for an indefinite period of time, alone and in the greatest peril ... I would be a swine indeed if, under those circumstances, I didn't do all in my power to offer you a helping hand—not merely in an official capacity, but in every capacity possible! You are angry that I don't recall your instructions? You have every right to be angry! I have a lousy memory, it's true. On the other hand, my superiors don't hold that against me. In our business, it's not healthy to remember too much. Suppose you're about to leave on your Mission and I happen to blurt out—unintentionally, of course—some detail, oh the most unimportant trifle. Yet, finding its way *there* through certain channels, it could prove fatal, destroy you. You understand? Isn't it better, then, for me to forget what passes through my hands? Otherwise, I'd have to be constantly on my guard, watch every word ... And then, it's not every day that someone loses his instructions! You can hardly blame me for not having prepared for that eventuality! We'll start disciplinary procedures against you, that can't be helped—but do get rid of these unfounded suspicions."

"Very well," I said. "I understand. At least, I'm trying to understand. But what about my instructions? Someone must have the originals!"

"Sure!" he answered with a characteristic toss of his blond hair. "The Commander in Chief has them in his safe. You need special permission to get at them, of course. Those things can't be done in a hurry. But it shouldn't take too long!" he added hastily.

"May I leave this with you?" I asked, placing my folder on his desk.

"What is it?"

"Didn't I tell you? It's the folder they switched on me."

"Ah, there you go again!"

He shook his head.

"I wonder," he said, half to himself, "if I shouldn't send you to Medicals . . ."

But he opened the folder and glanced at the plan and the map sewn together with white thread. He examined them. There was an odd look on his face.

"Peep," he muttered under his breath.

His bright eyes lifted and met mine.

"Mind if I leave you for a second? Just a second, I promise . . ."

I didn't protest, especially since he took the compromising documents with him. He went out by a side door, didn't even bother to shut it; I heard a chair move, and then a faint scratching sound. I got up, tiptoed over to the door, and peeked in.

Major Erms was sitting at a small desk under a bright lamp, guiding a pencil over a blank sheet of paper with the utmost care. He was copying out the plans of the Building. I moved closer, unable to believe my eyes. The floor creaked. Erms whirled around and saw me. He was startled at first, but quickly broke into a friendly grin.

"I didn't want to be rude," he said, getting up, "and work right in front of you . . . which is why . . ."

He tossed his sketch on the desk with an exaggerated

lack of concern. It skidded across the highly polished wood and almost fell to the floor. Erms handed me the original papers.

"No, you keep them," I mumbled, confused by the whole incident.

"And what would I do with them? No, they have to be submitted to the Registry. You're going there anyway to file a formal report on the loss of your instructions. I'd gladly take care of the matter for you, except that unfortunately this has to be done in person."

We returned to his office and sat down, facing each other across the desk.

"Then—the originals of my instructions? I have to wait until after the disciplinary action?" But before he could reply, I added, surprised that I was actually asking this:

"Why did you copy those plans?"

"Copy?" Major Erms shook his head. "You're imagining things. I was only checking their authenticity. There are so many fakes in circulation, you know."

I wanted to shout, "That's not true! I saw it! You were making a copy!" But all I could say was:

"They're fakes?"

"Well, I shouldn't be telling you this, but . . ." He leaned over with a conspiratorial air. "Everything's authentic except for the second and third levels . . . but keep that under your hat."

"Of course!" I said, and was about to leave when I remembered the meal tickets. He rummaged around for them, looked in his pockets and under his papers, cursing his forgetfulness, tossing out all sorts of personal odds and ends on the desk. Among them was a small, spotted stone.

I waited and watched him carefully. Was he telling the truth? I had seen with my own eyes how he copied the plans. What did it mean? Why would he do something like that?

Could it be that the head of the Department of Instructions was also working for . . . Really, what nonsense! This was not normal, healthy suspicion. Could I be on the brink of a nervous breakdown? My actions in the Admiral's office, for example, all that melodrama . . . Here was an old man who needed a nap at the end of a long and difficult day, who had a few blemishes common to old age, who collected animal cards—and I had to conjure up some diabolical plot out of all this! How absurd! Still, Major Erms did copy those plans, plans which had nothing to do with his Department—he said so himself—and which he was not even allowed to hold for me . . . Why didn't he at least close the door? Did he take me for a harmless idiot? That I doubted. Then why expose himself like that, unless . . .

Unless he considered me an ally, said a strange voice in my head. Suddenly, there was a shout: Major Erms had found my meal tickets, they were in his wallet.

"Here," he said, giving them to me. "Now go to 1116, that's the Registry, give them your papers and make your report. I'll phone ahead and let them know you're coming. But please, go straight there, don't get lost on the way!" He smiled and walked me to the door. I went meekly, my head filled with a hundred bewildering thoughts, and was already walking down the hall when he stuck his head out the door and yelled:

"Drop in later!"

I continued on my way. If he took me for an ally . . . then he had no fears I would expose him. I wasn't that familiar with the machinery of intelligence, but I did know that agents assigned to different territories usually couldn't identify one another. This was to minimize the possibility that some serious slip-up might uncover the whole operation, blow the entire network. On the basis of all the evidence against me, Major Erms could easily have taken me for one of his . . . though, on the other hand, he would be in no hurry to reveal himself to me. One thing didn't fit. If Major Erms was really working for the enemy, that is, if he was an infiltrator, a plant in the Department of Instructions, and if he really took me for someone working on his side, then surely he would warn me, let me know the score, not deliberately try to confuse me . . .

Just a minute! Was there ever such a thing as solidarity among agents? Everyone was out for himself, everyone had his own assignment. Major Erms would sacrifice me without a moment's hesitation, whether I was an ally or not, if that would strengthen his own position or in any way promote the success of whatever mission he had himself.

Yes, clearly he would. Then what could I do? Where could I turn? I'd left my book and papers in his office: that would be pretext enough. I hurried back, trying my best to assume an appropriately absentminded look. I went in without knocking.

Never in a hundred years would I have thought to catch him doing this!

Sitting back in his chair, legs propped up on the desk, and beating time on the coffee cup with his spoon, he was singing! Oh, he must have been thoroughly pleased with himself! Those plans he copied—what a windfall! He broke off when he saw me, not a bit embarrassed, and laughed.

"You caught me red-handed! Fooling around on the job! A man does what he can not to turn into a rubber stamp. Your book, right? Over there. You know, I admire you— even waiting around in reception rooms, you improve your mind. And don't forget the papers." I nodded and was about to leave, when a thought hit me.

"Sir?"

It was the first time I had called him "sir." He frowned. "Yes?"

"This whole conversation . . . it was in code, wasn't it?"

"But—"

"Code," I insisted, even managing a smile. "Right? Everything, everything is code!"

I left him standing behind the desk with his mouth open.

8

I practically ran from there, afraid he might follow in pursuit. Now why had I done that? To frighten him? How could he possibly fear me? I was helpless in a net, and he and others like him held the ends of it in their hands. Even so, I felt more confident—but why? After some thought, I came to the conclusion that I owed this moral boost to none other than Major Erms—it was not his empty chatter, his pretended sincerity, his displays of warmth and attention, things I had believed in for a while only because I needed to believe, but it was that scene I witnessed through the open door that encouraged me. For if, I reasoned, he was really one of *them* and held such a high position, then it was possible to fool, deceive, outsmart the Building, even in its most highly guarded strongholds. That meant the Building was far from infallible, that it was omniscient only in my imagination. A depressing discovery, in a way—yet it opened new and unexpected horizons.

Halfway to the Registry I had second thoughts. Major Erms had sent me there, so they expected me. I had to do something different, I had to break out of that vicious circle of planned activity. But where could I go? Nowhere, and he knew it. Except the bathroom. The bathroom wasn't that bad—I could think things over there in peace and quiet, try to make some sense out of it all, and I could shave. I needed a shave. The only reason they didn't stare at me in the hall was probably that they had orders not to.

I took an elevator up to the bathroom with the razor, got the razor and took it to my regular bathroom. But at the door I remembered something Major Erms had said, something about a *close shave*. Had he foreseen this eventuality? I stared at the white door. Should I go in or not? How could shaving have any effect on anything? Anyway, I could sit here as long as I wanted to, in solitude—they had no jurisdiction over the bathroom!

I entered cautiously: the place was vacant, as usual. But wasn't the lightbulb by the urinals a little brighter than before? I walked in, and almost immediately jumped back—there was a man lying alongside the tub, a towel rolled under his head for a pillow. My first impulse was to leave. But they were probably expecting me to do just that, so I decided to stay.

The man didn't stir, not even when I tripped over my feet and crashed into the sink; he was sound asleep. All I could see, from where I stood, was the top of his head, not enough to tell whether I knew him or not. Still, he looked like a stranger. He wore civilian clothes, had a jacket over his shoulders, a striped shirt with dirty cuffs under a thin sweater. One hand was tucked under his head, and the knees were drawn up to the chin. His breathing was deep and steady.

"Well," I thought, "there are other bathrooms. I can move wherever I want." Though the notion of moving was silly—what was there to move but myself?

Let him sleep, I could still shave; there was nothing subversive in that. I put the razor on the sink under the mirror, reached over the sleeping man to get the soap from the soap dish by the tub, then turned on the hot water and inspected myself in the mirror. The face of a derelict. My stubble made me look thinner; in another few days it would be on the way to a beard. I lathered up the skin as best I could without a brush and tried the razor: extremely sharp. Now shaving has always helped me think, and since the man on the floor didn't disturb me in the least, here was a good opportunity to come to grips with my predicament.

What had happened so far? General Kashenblade had entrusted me with a Special Mission when I went to see him, then there were the displays, the collections, my first guide was arrested, the second one vanished, I was left alone with an open safe, then there was the little old man with the gold spectacles, his suicide, another officer and *his* suicide, then the chapel with the corpse, the priest who gave me the number of Major Erms's office, then Prandtl, the flies in the coffee, the disappearance of my instructions, my despair, my accidental or—let's not jump to conclusions—unaccidental visit to the Archives, next the reception room of the Investigation Department, the Admiral, the Counter-decoration Ceremony, finally my second conversation with Major Erms. Those were, more or less, the incidents. Now the people involved . . . in order not to sink here into a hopeless mire of conjecture, I had to take something definite as my starting point, something concrete, indisputable, a clear fact. Death would serve. I began with the little old man in the gold spectacles.

He poisoned himself because he had taken me for someone else, a courier from *them;* he thought, since I didn't return his coded signals with the appropriate counter-signals, that I was sent to punish him for treason. Of course, he wasn't really an old man. There was no mistaking that shock of black hair beneath the wig. But the captain (the one who shot himself) kept referring to him as "old." Had the captain been lying, then? Not unlikely, especially in light of what followed. The captain's suicide definitely made his words suspect. He killed himself because he was afraid of me. The exposure of any relatively minor offense would not have driven him to take such a drastic step. Ergo, he had to be an agent for *them.* The little old man (let's continue to call him that—after all, he took his guise to the grave with him) was obviously one of *them.* Otherwise, his suspicions and his loyalty would have demanded he turn me in, hand me over to the authorities. He took poison instead. Both deaths were quite real, undeniable—I saw them myself. So there was no doubt that both the little old man and the captain were enemy agents, the first less important, a mere pawn, the second quite important, considering his high position. Now the captain, assuming I was an investigator from Headquarters, quickly denounced the little old man to me, who was dead anyhow at the time of our conversation. He tried to explain why he hadn't denounced the little old man earlier in the game, pleading personal ambition and an overzealous dedication to the Cause. But when he saw that I wasn't buying this (actually, I simply didn't understand his code), there was nothing left but to shoot himself.

Though this interpretation of the two suicides made sense, it didn't settle the question of my role in the whole episode. That is, had it all been worked out in advance, or was my appearance in those two offices a tragic accident?

"Let's go on," I thought. "This analysis may yet lead to something."

I finished shaving, wiped off the lather, splashed cold water on my face. I felt almost cheerful. My reasoning demonstrated that not everything in the Building was incomprehensible; I had managed to piece together at least a part of the puzzle. Drying my face with a rough towel, I noticed the man on the floor—I had completely forgotten him. Yes, he was still asleep. Having no intention now of going to the Registry, and hardly eager to continue my wandering from corridor to corridor, I sat on the edge of the tub, leaned back against the tiled wall, drew my knees up, and returned to my thoughts.

Major Erms, friendly Major Erms. There was trouble there. Even if he wasn't out to double-cross the Building, I couldn't trust him. For all his great show of sincerity, not a peep about my Mission. He either gave me compliments I didn't deserve or dealt in generalities that said nothing. When pressed, he did give me my instructions. But then they were stolen in Prandtl's office. That was really the important thing, the instructions themselves, not Major Erms. If he gave them to me, knowing they wouldn't be in my possession long, then it was only to let me take a look . . .

And were those papers the real instructions? Real instructions would have been addressed to me, would have presented plans, suggested lines of action, and certainly would have given the scope, the essence of the Mission. But they looked more like memoirs, the memoirs of a man lost in the Building! A code? What sort of code would look like that?

Well, perhaps, if I were to believe Prandtl. Even Shakespeare could be deciphered, according to Prandtl. Though I had only his word for it. I hadn't really seen any decoding machine, just a hand, and tape coming out of a hole in the wall.

Better not be too skeptical—there was nowhere left to go, that way. And that peculiar sigh in my face, as if Prandtl had something to tell me, but didn't dare—the sigh, the expression in his eye?

That couldn't be dismissed. There was more than human compassion in that sigh—perhaps an awareness of my predicament, knowledge of what the Building had in store for me. Prandtl was the only one I'd met who stepped outside the rule of official impersonality, having first alluded to its burden.

Yet was it really so surprising that Prandtl should know what was planned for me? Even without the sigh, it was perfectly clear that I had been summoned to the Building and chosen for the Mission—for some definite purpose. A mighty revelation! Really, was this the best I could do?

The sleeping man groaned and turned over, covering most of his face with his jacket. After which he was still again and breathing evenly.

I watched him for a while, then gradually returned to the idea I had had—for how long?—forever, it seemed—the idea that all of this, even now, was still a test, a fantastically prolonged and involved test.

Seen in that light, so much of what had puzzled me now fell into place—especially the continual postponement of my Mission, as if they were checking me out thoroughly first, seeing how I'd react in totally unexpected and confusing situations, testing my personal endurance as well, toughening me up, preparing me for the real thing. Naturally every precaution had to be taken to hide this from me; once I guessed that these situations were simulated and therefore harmless, the entire test would be ruined and the training made worthless.

Yet I had guessed! Were my powers of observation a cut above the normal? Suddenly I shuddered, almost slipping off the tub: I had found the common thread that ran through all these incidents . . .

In the course of only a few hours, almost at every step since I entered the Building, I had come into contact with enemy agents. First the guide they arrested in the hall after he took me through the collections, then the pale spy with the camera at the open safe, then the little old man with the gold spectacles, and the captain who shot himself, not to mention Major Erms, a prime suspect—five agents in all, five conspirators revealed—and in so short a time! It was more than incredible—it was impossible! It was impossible for the Building to be in such a state of decay, so completely, so massively infiltrated. One agent alone would make you stop and think—but four or five? Utterly beyond the realm of possibility. There had to be something behind it. A test, a staging. But that theory didn't satisfy me. A swarm of enemy agents, open safes full of secret documents, spies around every corner—that could all be staged for my benefit, yes. But the deaths? I remembered only too well those final convulsions, the death rattle, the cooling of the body—how could I possibly doubt the authenticity of those deaths? Nor would deaths be ordered up as part of the deception—not that the Building was motivated by compassion, nothing of the kind! But purely for the most practical reasons: it was unthinkable to sacrifice the lives of well-placed and high-grade operatives simply to train another recruit, a candidate. No new agent was worth the loss of two pros.

My theory collapsed in the face of those two deaths, it

had no choice. No choice? . . . How many times, traveling aimlessly here and there like a speck of dust in the wind, driven like a blade of grass in a stream, never knowing what the next moment would bring, sometimes submitting to events, sometimes resisting them—how many times had I been forced to admit, always too late, that in any case I always ended up *exactly* where they wanted me? I was a billiard ball aimed with mathematical precision; my every move was plotted out, my every thought, even *this* thought, this sudden sense of futility, this dizziness, that enormous, invisible eye pointed at me now, watching everywhere, and all the doors waiting for me only to shut in my face, the phones waiting for me only to go dead, my questions remaining unanswered, and the whole Building united against me! Ah, and when I was ready to break, explode, go mad, they came and comforted me, kind and sympathetic—only to let me know later, unexpectedly, through some allusion or incident, that all my secrets were known to them. Major Erms ordered me to report to the Registry, knowing full well I would defy him and head for the bathroom instead— and that was why I found this man here and was now killing time, waiting for him to wake up.

Yet why did the Building practically admit at the same time that its entire structure was infested with *them,* that apparently nothing could stem that fatal infiltration? Or was this cancer of treason only a figment of my imagination? The product of a disordered mind?

It was time to examine myself. In the beginning I had assumed that I was singled out, selected for something unusual. The obstacles in my way? Merely administrative errors; inconvenient, annoying, but no great cause for concern—unavoidable in any bureaucracy. When my instructions proved elusive, I resorted to bolder and bolder tactics (and got away with them), tactics which were not always clean (since I was convinced that honesty had no place here)—I had presented myself as an emissary from high up to obtain vital information, for example, or I had used, like a stolen weapon, those ominous code numbers which drove the captain to his suicide—and my lies had escalated as I pursued my goal, then as I began to avoid my goal, then as I turned about and fled from my goal—they were almost second nature to me now.

Though everything had been a lie, an illusion. But I pretended not to notice and plowed ahead, seeking some sign, some unmistakable proof of my Mission—though it had begun to dawn on me that there was no little dishonor in the honor of having a Mission, if I had to play dirty tricks, hide under desks, witness violent deaths, and then be hounded, ensnared, forced to invent one ridiculous explanation after another!

Deceived and robbed of everything, including my instructions and even the hope of their existence, I tried to explain, to justify myself—but since no one would listen, not even to catch me at my lies, the burden of the crimes I hadn't committed began to weigh so heavily upon me that I soon was prepared to accept this role of criminal, if only to make it a reality, to have my sentence and punishment over and done with. I sought out judges, not to plead my case but to confess, confess to everything and anything. It hadn't worked. In the Admiral's office I had played the traitor according to what I imagined a traitor to be, I planted the most incriminating evidence, rifled the drawers, ripped out their false bottoms—in vain.

In all of this, whether trusting and believing, if only for a moment, in the Mission and my instructions, or having my hopes dashed, even the hope of my own destruction— in all of this, I had been seeking some reason, good or bad, for my presence here. But neither indications of favor nor suspicions of treachery had seemed to make the least bit of difference. Again and again I was given to understand that nothing, really, was expected of me. And that was the only thing I couldn't accept, because it didn't make sense.

Begin at the beginning: what if there were no staging, no test, no masquerade, but this were the Mission itself, my Special Mission?

For a brief moment, that thought was like the opening of

109

a door—I didn't dare examine it, only closed my eyes and listened to the pounding of my heart.

The Mission? Why should they hide it from me, then, why not simply tell me that my work would take me somewhere inside the Building, or that I was to keep certain people under surveillance? And why not brief me fully on what had to be done—instead of sending me out blindly, destination unknown, assignment unknown? If I ever accomplished anything, it would have to be an accident.

That's how it looked, on the surface of it. On the other hand the Building had familiarized me, to some degree at least, with its methods—confusing at times, but not without certain salient features. There were departments, sections, archives, offices, receptionists, regulations, ranks, phones, all cemented by an absolute obedience into one monolithic, hierarchic structure. It was rigid, well-regulated, ever vigilant, like the white corridors with their symmetrical rows of doors, like the offices with their scrupulously kept files; the communication systems were its entrails, the steel safes its hearts, and its veins and arteries were the pneumatic mail tubes that maintained a constant flow of secrecy. Nothing was overlooked, even the plumbing played a vital part. But underneath that surface of clockwork precision lay a hive of intrigue, skulduggery, deception. What exactly was that wild confusion? A game? Or perhaps a camouflage to prevent the uninitiated from seeing some deeper plan, some higher order . . .

Could it be that my muddled, erratic behavior was exactly what they wanted? A weapon which the Building directed against its enemies? Indeed, though all unwittingly and only (it would seem) by dumb luck, I had rendered some service to the Cause! I had taken both the little old man and the captain out of action; in many other cases I had probably functioned as a catalyst, bringing certain situations to a head or turning the balance in the Building's favor . . . Then I thought about the duplicity of all the people I had met—one might almost conclude that playing both sides was the general rule here—with two exceptions, the spy at the open safe and Prandtl.

There was no doubt about that spy. When even death had let me down—the behavior of the corpse under the flag was clearly ambiguous—at least the spy was left. He didn't toy with treason, didn't pretend, didn't play games. Once at the safe, he photographed documents, conscientiously pale and frightened. That was the sort of thing one expected from an honest spy.

Prandtl was not so easy. My trust in him was founded wholly on a sigh. Major Erms had said Prandtl would coach me in connection with the Mission. But my conversation with Prandtl turned out to be entirely different—though now I wasn't so sure about that either. Prandtl had said a great deal that wasn't clear, but assured me I would understand it all later. Did later mean *now*? . . .

It was also possible that Prandtl had no idea what was in store for me, nor cared, that his gesture of compassion was prompted not by any knowledge of my future, but by what had happened, that is, the reading of that final message after successive decodings, the scrap of paper with those five words.

They were in response to a question I had posed in my thoughts while waiting in the office, alone with the fat officer . . .

If everything that happened in the Building was supposed to have some deeper meaning, then there was more to Prandtl's sigh than met the eye.

I had asked: "What do they want me to do?"

And Prandtl handed me a piece of paper that said: "There will be no answer."

If there was no answer forthcoming to my questions, then everything—the Commander in Chief's promises, the open safe, my blackmail of Father Orfini, the shoot-out in the hall, the suicides, the missions, the instructions, the secret codes—absolutely everything was a maze of blunders, idiocies and horrors, everything fell apart, nothing held together, and the Building itself became a vacuum filled exclusively with lunatics, each kept in isolation . . . each hallucinating its omniscience and omnipotence . . .

But if these events were in fact unrelated, haphazard, thrown together any which way, having no pattern, no connection with anything else, then they were meaningless, and my visit with Prandtl was meaningless, and his lecture, and those five terrible words . . .

Those words lost their broader meaning and became, as at first, only one example in a demonstration of code. Now, if they had no broader meaning, and were therefore not in answer to my unspoken question, in that case . . . in that case there was a Building after all, and a mystery, and everything did have a deeper meaning and I was back where I started, describing a vicious circle of thought, of thought that devoured thought.

I glanced at the sleeping man. He breathed so quietly that if it hadn't been for the slight movement of his shoulders, I would have thought him dead. Perhaps I too was asleep—that might explain my failure to think all this through. No, I was wide awake.

Let us assume, for the moment, that those five words could be taken at face value, ignoring the above paradox. Where would this lead us? (Probably nowhere, but it would at least kill time.) Consider the possible usefulness of the chaos those words implied, a chaos that could be kept in check by various and devious means, turned almost into a tool. What purpose did chaos serve?

Here I was, given a Special Mission, chosen, singled out; then, with equal eagerness, I had assumed the role of criminal, the defendant in court, with all the trappings of confession, the sobs of remorse, the pleas for mercy; or else I had draped myself in the robes of martyr and made a desperate search for interrogators, prosecutors, was acquitted and rehabilitated, then found guilty and recondemned; on one hand I had rifled desks and files to find evidence I could use against myself, and on the other hand stormed offices with all the righteous indignation of an honest citizen grievously wronged. All this I had done with great spirit, conscientiously, convinced that that was what they expected of me. The Building, however, had been designed to get at the root of things, to unearth, unmask, penetrate appearances, layers of deception—and it accomplished this through dissonance. In my case, it destroyed the harmony of defeat as well as the harmony of heroism, it led me from one rude awakening to another, jolted me, amazed me so that I would be unable to read anything in the many favors and misfortunes that rained down in turn upon my head, and then it threw me into an acid bath of chaos and calmly waited to see what would emerge, purged and purified.

Precisely by denying me both my instructions and a warrant for my arrest, both medals and manacles, precisely by using its vast resources, its hundred corridors and hoards of desks, to give me *nothing*—the Building was nearing its goal . . .

Yes, chaos could be useful . . .

And the little old man with the gold spectacles—hadn't he said something about an infinite variety of operational plans?

From there it was only one step to concluding that chaos in the Building was not only not unusual, but actually the norm—more, the result of considerable effort, continual diligence. It was an artificial chaos, forged to shield the Ultimate Secret from prying eyes.

Perhaps . . . I shifted my weary weight on the hard rim of the tub. My other theories also fit a lot of the facts. Odd, how almost any sufficiently complex idea seemed to apply to the Building, to explain it . . . Odd, and a little frightening.

The sleeping man moved over on his back, so I could see his face. The eyelids flickered—he seemed to be reading something in his sleep, the eyeballs moved from left to right. Sweat glistened on his brow; he badly needed a shave, and was deathly pale, with a twisted smile—no, a frown, a grimace (the face was upside down from where I sat).

I'd wait for him to wake up and say something . . . and

somewhere in some office a bored secretary had stirred her coffee and was now getting up to file a folder of instructions, instructions that contained exactly what he would say to me when he opened his eyes, and what I would say to him, and so on—to the bitter end.

I felt a sudden chill, either from this morbid thought or from the draft that ran across the tub, and pulled my knees up closer and buttoned the top button of my jacket.

What difference did it make, I reasoned, tired and defeated. They'd never show me those instructions, if only to keep me from going against them, and so my future remained unknown to me, almost as if it hadn't been written down in any ledger anywhere . . .

9

The sleeping man began to snore—not with the Admiral's virtuosity, but in a stubborn monotone. Soon he was sawing away with a dedication worthy of a better cause. Evidently he had decided to imitate the sounds of a dying man. This unnerved me, I couldn't concentrate any more—an attempt to divert my attention? I was tired, my bones ached. Once again I decided to leave, go somewhere, perhaps visit that old hermit—no, on second thought, it was too crowded there. I stretched, went over to the sink, put the razor in my pocket. In the mirror I saw the sleeping man, from the chest up; it was like looking at myself sound asleep after some long and wearisome journey.

Could it be that this hadn't been arranged? That I had found a genuine companion, a fellow sufferer, someone as lost in the Building as I was, chasing a similar mirage?

I could tell by the sudden silence that he was beginning to wake up. He stirred slowly, with great effort, as if carefully putting away his pretense of dying, saving it for another time. The eyes flashed open, took me in (upside down), then shut for a moment, while he collected his thoughts. Finally, he lifted himself up on one elbow. Before he spoke, I seemed to recall something—I had seen that face before. Eyes still shut, he muttered:

"Tailed . . ."

"I beg your pardon?"

He sat up, scratched his head, blinked, looked at me, looked at the floor, then coughed and said, rubbing his wrists:

"That cauliflower . . . the bastards don't cook it right, gives you nightmares . . ."

He glanced at the sink—I was in the way—he leaned around me and his eyes widened.

"All right, where's the razor?" he asked.

"Here." I pointed to my pocket.

"Hand it over."

"Why?" I objected, already taking a dislike to the man. He was too arrogant. Wherever I had seen him before, I was sure it hadn't been pleasant.

"I brought it here, from upstairs," I said, establishing my rights to it. He gave me a nasty look, turned his back to me and got up. He stretched and scratched his shoulders leisurely, with obvious pleasure. Then he took a brush off the shelf and started to remove the lint from his trousers.

"Go on!" he growled, not looking at me.

"What?"

"Look, either talk—or get lost!"

"Talk about what?"

The sound of my voice stopped him. He looked up and frowned.

"All right," he said, and came up to me with his hand out, palm up. "Well, what are you waiting for? Scared?"

"I'm not scared of you," I said, giving him the razor. He weighed it in his hand and looked me over carefully.

"Of me?" he repeated. "I guess not . . ."

He hung his jacket on the doorknob, wrapped a towel around his neck and proceeded to lather his face. Having nothing else to do, I sat on the rim of the tub and watched. He ignored me. Then I happened to notice a leather loop sticking out from under the tub. Suddenly it hit me: this was the spy with the camera! Of course! *They* sent him, sent him in order to . . . to what? We would soon see. He would make his pitch any minute now. The silence was painful. The tips of my shoes touched the floor and, as sometimes happens in an awkward position, my left leg began to dance.

"Been here . . . long?" I asked, trying to sound casual.

All I could see in the mirror was a lot of lather, no face. I waited for an answer. But the razor slid from ear to chin as if I hadn't said a thing.

"Have you been here long?" I asked again.

"Go on," he said, scraping under his chin.

"Go on?" I said, baffled. He didn't explain, but only bent over the sink and splashed his face, splashing me in the process.

"You're splashing me," I told him.

"You don't like it? Then get lost!"

"I was here first."

An eye regarded me from behind the towel.

"Oh?" he countered. "Really?"

"Yes."

He tossed the towel on the floor and reached for his jacket, saying:

"Supper over?"

"I don't know."

"No meat today," he mumbled to himself, straightening his clothes. "If only they'd give us French fries for a change. But no, it's mashed potatoes, it's always mashed potatoes. Coming out of my ears . . ."

He cast a quick glance at me.

"Are you going to start or not? I'm about ready to leave."

"Start what?"

"Don't play innocent. That's old hat."

"You're the one who's playing innocent."

"Me?" He seemed surprised. "How do you figure that?"

"You know how."

"We could go on this way forever," he said impatiently, then took another close look at me. There was absolutely no doubt: he was the one I had seen photographing the secret documents in the open safe.

"In mufti, eh?" he said with a grin.

"What do you mean?"

He came up very close and looked at my dancing leg. It interested him.

"A stool pigeon," he decided at last.

"Who?"

"You."

"Me? Look, why don't you talk sense? I'm not in mufti and I'm no stool pigeon!"

"Oh? Then what are you doing here? Just happened by?"

"No, I didn't just happen by!"

"Then what do you want?"

"You're the one who wants something."

"Me?"

He paced the bathroom floor from one end to the other, hands in his pockets. Then he stopped at the door and said:

"All right, so I made a mistake. And you're not a decoder?"

"No."

"Not a forty?"

"What's that?"

He let out a long, low whistle.

"All right. I don't believe you, but we'll let that pass. So you say you're one of them mission people?"

I hesitated.

"I'm not sure I know what you mean," I began. "If you're talking about my Mission . . ."

"Ha," he said. "You got your instructions?"

"Yes, but—"

"Lost them?"

"Yes. Perhaps you know—"

"Hold on."

He bent down, reached under the tub and pulled out a camera in a large leather case. Then he sat on the toilet, opened the camera and took out a package of cookies.

"Missed supper," he explained, his mouth full and dropping crumbs. "So you want to know what's going on?"

"Yes."

"Was there a priest?"

"Yes."

"Lily white?"

"What?"

"Haven't gotten there yet, eh? All right. Looks like an eighty."

And he stared at my leg, which was still shaking, and calculated something.

You saw the old man," he concluded. "And the fat one too, eh? What a slob! You don't have to say a word, it's written all over your face. And the leg, that's from the old man."

He held out a cookie.

"Hungry?"

"No, thanks."

He shifted his weight on the toilet, made himself comfortable.

"You got a good look, didn't you?" he said sadly. "Quarts of warts and moles like coals, scroffles like waffles, and lumps and lumps, a bumper crop all right—and there you stand, spick-and-span, pearls before swine, a bull in a china shop! He whispers in your shell-like ear, a voice from the burning bush, and there you go, figuring, wriggling, and you can't make a thing out of it nohow. Still a test? Going west? House arrest?"

"Excuse me," I said, "but I don't—"

"Still a test," he decided. "But you're sharp, you get by! What a guy! Riding high! Too young to die! And did they stick you with pins in your sleep?"

"No. But why are you—"

"Don't interrupt. Artificial flies in your coffee?"

"Yes!"

I had no idea where all this was leading; yet it did make some sense, and clearly had to do with me.

"Were you talking about the Admiral just then?" I asked.

"No, apple strudel . . . The old boy will outlive us both, you know. He was exactly the same way back when you couldn't get a towel for love or money—and a razor, that was impossible . . . Coffee too . . . And they took care of you without all these rights and grounds today—good old cloak-and-dagger, everything hush-hush, a knock at the door and a visit to the Cellar Section, a little slapping around, a little boot in the kisser, a tooth or two, sign here and you're through. The most they do now is have an occasional shoot-out."

"Yes! In the hall! But why?"

"A three-timer. Tried to defect, got confused. They had to make an example of him. That's why."

Just an ordinary run-of-the-mill spy! It was obvious, the way he talked. But what did he want of me? Apparently giving up his supper to have a chat . . . I had to be on my guard!

"On your guard, eh?" he snapped and looked me in the eye. "Don't be so surprised, I'm an old hand at this game, run-of-the-mill or not. You think your instructions are yours? Wrong! One in a series, that's all . . . the flies in the coffee, and all the rest of it . . . Only the coffee hasn't changed . . ."

Suddenly he looked very old and tired, his eyes fixed on the gleaming white door.

"Can't you speak more clearly?" I asked.

"How could it be any clearer?" he replied, surprised.

"But what does it all really mean? And you—what are you trying to—"

"Easy, relax. Why worry over spilt milk? Am I a spot to be removed? A blot to be erased? A stain to be rubbed out? And do we not bleed? But enough, 'tis the end."

"The end of what?"

"Everything. In the good old days, you'd sniff a rose, your heart would skip a beat: bugged or not? And goose flesh—is your goose cooked or not? Shivers down your spine—cold feet? Every terror had a terror then . . . Nowadays, if you tremble, it's only out of habit . . . nothing but window dressing now."

"What are you getting at? Why a rose, why cold feet? You mean—my leg? And what is that supposed to mean? And—what are you doing here, anyway?"

"He wants to know what I'm doing here . . ." He leaned over and pointed to his own face. "Look what they've done to me! Those hordes of idiot spies, the paperwork, the waiting in offices, all that monkey business—ruined me!"

"Why the camera?" I asked, throwing all caution to the winds.

"The camera? You don't know?"

"You were taking pictures . . ."

"Of course."

"In the safe . . ." I lowered my voice to a whisper, still hoping he might deny it. But he nodded gravely.

"That goes without saying. Though it was quite harmless. I only did it to keep my hand in. Otherwise you get rusty, the gray matter rots, the old giblets cake up—every so often I just have to go and click the shutter a few times or I'll go mad."

"Don't give me that!" I said, suddenly impatient. "You were photographing secret documents! I saw you! Not that I have any intention of making use of this information—it's none of my business. What I don't understand is how you can just sit there."

"Why not?"

"They might be after you, you ought to hide!"

"Where?" he asked. The weariness in his voice gave me the shivers.

"Well, there's always . . . *there*."

I was putting myself in his hands. My heart hammered wildly. Now surely that boredom would fall from his face like a mask. I was urging him to escape—had I gone mad? —why, he could be an agent provocateur . . .

"*There?*" he muttered. "There's no *there*. Here, there— no difference. I took the pictures to keep my hand in, that's all. It doesn't matter anyway."

"Doesn't matter? Can't you speak more plainly?"

"Plainly or not, it all works out the same. You're not far enough along to understand. And even if you knew your p's and q's, you'd never believe them. I know what you're thinking: he's a spy, provocateur, sent by *them,* out to get me, blackmail, a regular snake, pretending to be sick of it all, lackaday and alas, all woebegone, baring his soul, run-down by the old run-around, the poor dear, but it's all a front, means something else—right? And now you're thinking, he says he's a spy to make me think he's being honest. But of course 'being honest' means something else to them, so when he says he's a spy to show me he's 'being honest,' then we know where we stand, don't we? Or do we? And now you don't believe a word I'm saying! Right?"

I said nothing.

"You'll see. You won't be spared a thing. Still want to know what's what, eh?"

He waited for my answer.

"I do!" I said, though I really didn't believe a word he was saying.

He made a bitter, twisted smile.

"You don't believe me—all right! At least you're trying. Listen. First they lined up for the bread, once upon a time. The last seat, toilet or otherwise, was taken. Full house. Afterwards—quit when the money's still coming in? Then they couldn't quit. Plant, infiltrate, fake, doctor, drug! Under the rug! Double agents, all right—triples, fine— quadruples, okay—and then quintuples come out of the woodwork! Lord knows how long this has been going on! An epidemic! A plague! Me, I tell you this, an honest, decent spy of the old school—me you can believe!"

And he beat his breast.

"Wait a second," I said, "I'm not sure I understand. Are you trying to say—"

"I'm not trying to say anything—can't you understand that? What, I should spill my guts? Are you a phonograph needle to my worn-out record? Must you magnify every sound, split every hair, turn every word upside down, inside out, look in the lining of every syllable, and my snoring, the soap, the razor—must everything be an allusion? All right, do what you will—just keep away from the razor! You have time yet. Things would be too easy if you could have the razor right off. You know, when I first saw you I thought you were sent to take it away."

"But I brought it here, from upstairs! It isn't yours, is it?"

"Like I say, you have time yet. Above all, keep up your

strength. Regular meals, an occasional snack, cookies and milk, some cake . . . What's the matter? You think that when I say 'cake,' I mean something, like maybe Headquarters or your instructions? Forget it! Cake is cake, period—at least with me. And no one sent me. I slept, I shaved, I missed supper on account of you, and now I'm off. See, I told you everything you wanted to know, and you don't believe a word of it! Not a word, right? I spill my guts, give you the real dope on all these espials and cabals, and you go and make another puzzle out of it."

He got up.

"So you're not a spy?"

"Who says I'm not? Who says I am? Give me something spiable, why don't you! No, I've had it. It's always the same—and for what? For whom? I'm through, the good guy, the simple soul, the individualist, my song is sung. What do they take me for, an onion? Now even sextuples are turning up. When you get over your suspicions, drop in. Tomorrow, after supper. All right?"

"All right," I said.

"See you. Stiff upper lip. I'm off to find a snack bar."

At the door he added over his shoulder:

"Next on the agenda is the doctor, plates, and then lily white. After the plates, you receive spiritual comfort. Then more monkey business. If I'm not here, wait. I'll come for sure."

"I'll wait."

He shut the door behind him. I heard his footsteps recede, another door open and close, then silence. They had put a lid on me, to bring me to a boil that much faster.

10

So . . . I had considered myself the center of the universe, the bull's-eye, so to speak, for all the slings and arrows the Building had to offer—and all along I was nothing, just one of a series, another copy, a stereotype, trembling in all the places my predecessors trembled, repeating like a record player exactly the same words, feelings, thoughts. My melodramatic actions, the sudden impulses, false starts, surprises, moments of inspiration, each successive revelation—all of it, chapter and verse, including this present moment, was in the instructions—no longer *my* instructions, they weren't made for *me* . . . So if this was neither a test nor a Mission, nor chaos—what was left? The bathroom? The corridors? Going from door to door, from door to door . . .

Why had he told me so much? He too, of course, was part of the instructions, appearing like a note in a musical score, a note whose turn had come. And he played it well, the old veteran! But why? Where was all this heading?

I slid down from the tub and lay on the floor for a while, my feet propped up on the toilet. How disgusting it all was! Quadruples, triplets . . . What did it mean? Maybe nothing, just a diversion. Diversion from what? Apple strudel, window dressing, burning bushes—it made me dizzy. And what about that cauliflower that gave one nightmares? And eating regularly, cookies and milk and cake and onions . . . Were they all crazy? Were they out to make me crazy too? Then everything would be fine, for if everyone's crazy, no one's crazy . . . But where was it all heading?

I looked at my watch: stopped. Even it had betrayed me. I tore it off my wrist and tossed it into the toilet. Let the Sanitation Department fish it out and examine it . . . Where was the razor? He had taken it, robbed me—trying to provoke me to—to do what? Yes, of course! Perfect! Full speed ahead!

I left the bathroom, whistling. I smiled at all the officers I passed. I took an elevator. No one in the corridor upstairs. So much the better. So much the worse. I entered the office.

Empty, not a sign of Major Erms. I went to his desk, yanked the drawers out, turned them upside down, shook everything out onto the floor, onto the chair, papers everywhere, a whirling cloud of paper. The door squeaked open and I saw Major Erm's face, his blue eyes wide with surprise.

"What—what are you doing?"

"You bastard!" I roared, lunging at him. We fell and rolled through secret documents—I had him by the throat, I kicked him, I bit him, but it was all over in a moment. People came running up, someone pulled me back by the collar, someone else threw a cup of cold coffee in my face, and Major Erms got up, pale and shaking, and they helped him gather up his papers. I spat out a couple of ribbons I had bitten off his jacket and shrieked while they held me down:

"Finish me off, villains, dogs! Finish me off! Yes, I plotted, I conspired! I am an agent of a foreign power! I aided, I abetted, I committed treason! Yes! I confess! Shoot me! Torture me! Finish me off!!"

Several people passed by the open door, but no one looked in, even though I was bellowing at the top of my lungs. Finally, thoroughly hoarse and exhausted, I could only gasp like a fish out of water. Someone in white approached me from the side, rolled up the sleeve of my jacket; I saw a moon face with glasses, felt something stab my arm, then an odd warmth spreading out . . .

"Tallyho!" I cried as everything faded away. "Bless you, murderers, bless you!"

I came to slowly, by degrees. I was enormous. Not that

I had become a giant; my body hadn't grown. But I, the I who was now thinking, was a space equivalent in volume to the space surrounding me, if not larger. I didn't move a muscle, yet my inner being encompassed the myriad levels of the white labyrinth. Snugly ensconced in the warm depths of myself, between my powerful walls, I considered my recent trials and tribulations with infinite patience and pity.

Gradually I dwindled, tightened up, somehow returned to my old self. I was lying on a hard uncomfortable bed. I moved my fingers—they stuck together. The coffee thrown at me must have had sugar in it. I lifted my head. It wobbled, as if it hadn't been properly screwed on. I sat up and leaned against a cold, tiled wall.

This wasn't a bathroom. I was on a vinyl couch, fairly high off the ground. The room was long and narrow, had white chairs and a folding screen at one end. I could see the corner of a small desk behind the screen. On a metal cart at my side were medicine bottles, a hypodermic syringe, assorted surgical instruments. Obviously, a doctor's office. Then I recalled what had just happened. So instead of throwing me in jail, they were treating me? What next?

Still in a daze, I tried to figure out why there were only ten bottles on the cart when there were supposed to be nineteen. At the same time I knew perfectly well that this didn't make any sense.

Someone behind the screen was looking at me; I saw the top of a head and the glint of glasses. It was the doctor who had given me the injection.

"How are you feeling?" he asked, coming out.

"Fine, thanks."

A small man in white, on the plump side, eager to please, pink complexion. There were dark, intelligent eyes behind those thick, horn-rimmed glasses. The nose was a round button, and there was a dimple in the chin. In the opening of his white coat I could see a green polka dot tie, and when he came nearer, the lapels of a uniform. He pulled up a stool next to my couch, sat down and took my pulse.

"I'm all right," I said when he brought out a stethoscope from the pocket of his coat.

"Of course," he replied in a smooth and pleasant voice. "Do you remember everything?"

"Yes."

"Wonderful! That's a very good sign. You are going through a most difficult, a most complicated period— adjusting to a new environment, etc. Many things disturb the equilibrium, and then there's all that secrecy to contend with, how our psyche hates it! We have a stubborn, rebellious nature; the minute it is presented with anything forbidden, all hell breaks loose, you see. A perfectly normal reaction, though—er—not exactly encouraged around here. We can help you."

"How?" I asked. I still had on my trousers and shirt. But my jacket was hanging on the wall and someone had taken off my shoes. I felt stupid without them.

"You're an intelligent man," he said with a broad smile, making a dimple in his left cheek. "And intelligence demands a certain skepticism—a normal, healthy skepticism. Now, we're not omnipotent, Lord knows . . . if you don't object, of course, we could sit down and have a little talk. Just between us, you understand. But perhaps you'd like to wash up first? A bath?"

"That's a good idea. I'm sticky from that coffee . . ."

"Ah, let's not even mention that—incident. I'll just say that the Major did ask me to tell you that he fully understands—and there'll be no trouble on that score, none whatsoever."

"What?" I asked dully. He blinked.

"That little, uh, scene we had . . . You lost your temper, one might say you even lost your head—there were certain disappointments, I suppose. We needn't go into it. But the Major asked me to give you a few words of encouragement. He thinks quite highly of you, you know . . ."

"You said something about a bath?" I interrupted, beginning to feel not unlike that spy in the bathroom. I got down from the couch. Whatever was in the injection had completely worn off. The doctor directed me through a side door to the bathroom. I hung my clothes up in a little closet, gave myself a good scrubbing, then took a cold shower. Feeling worlds better, I threw on a loose bathrobe which was folded over a chair nearby, went back to the closet and found it empty. Just then, I heard a cautious knock.

"It's me," came the doctor's voice from behind the door. "Can I come in?"

I opened the door.

"My clothes," I said, confronting him.

"Oh yes, I forgot to tell you. The nurse took them to sew on a button, or maybe they needed some ironing."

"Searching without a warrant?" I asked, unconcerned. He flinched.

"Still some traces of shock," he muttered to himself. "I'll prescribe a tranquilizer for you, yes. And now, if you don't mind, I'll examine you."

I let him test my reflexes and listen to my heart. He nodded vigorously.

"Wonderful," he exclaimed. "You're in splendid shape. Now let's go to my office. The nurse will bring your clothes presently. This way, please."

We went down a narrow hall to a dim room with a green lamp on the desk and massive bookcases filled with volumes bound in leather, the titles all in gold. Near one bookcase stood a round table with a skull in the middle, and two armchairs.

I took a seat—the books behind the glass seemed to breathe gloom. The doctor hung up his white coat and I saw that he wasn't in uniform after all, but was wearing an ordinary gray suit. He sat across the table from me and watched me carefully for a considerable time.

"And now," he said at last, as if my face had passed inspection, "perhaps we can discuss what prompted that little—that little outburst of yours. In the privacy of my office, of course." And he indicated the long, dark rows of books with a wave of the arm.

"Feel free to tell me everything."

He waited for me to start. When I didn't, he said:

"You don't trust me. Perfectly natural. I would feel the same in your place, I'm sure. But believe me, you *must* try to overcome this compulsion to be silent. It's important that you try. The first step is always the most difficult."

"That's not it," I said. "The thing is, I don't know if it's really worth it ... Anyway, you took me by surprise— just a while ago you were saying that you didn't want to hear about it."

"You must forgive me," he said, showing his dimples. "Before anything else, I am a doctor. In the other room I wasn't sure you had completely recovered, I didn't want to excite you by stirring up painful memories. But now that I've examined you, I know that I not only can, but that I should—of course, I don't insist, but if you're willing to cooperate ..."

"Very well," I said, "I'll talk. But it's a long story."

"I'm all ears."

What was there to lose? I began at the beginning, summarized my interview with the Commander in Chief, told about the Mission, my instructions, all the complications, told him about the little old man, the officers, the priest, all my suspicions (except those touching Major Erms), also about the spy sleeping in the bathroom and our odd conversation—but I no longer followed what I was saying, having realized that without mention of the fact that I had caught Major Erms copying secret documents, my attack on him appeared insane. So I tried to find some aspects of my conversation with the spy in the bathroom which might justify, at least to some extent, my mad behavior. But my arguments were unconvincing even to myself, and the more I talked, the less I seemed to say, yet I plowed on grimly, getting in deeper and deeper, convinced that I was only providing additional evidence that I was not in full possession of my senses.

While I talked, the doctor picked up the skull (it served as a paperweight) and put it down in different positions:

sometimes it was in profile to me, sometimes it stared at me with its gaping eyes. When I finished, he sat back in his chair, clasped his hands and said in a smooth voice:

"As far as I can see, your doubts concerning the importance and, for that matter, the very existence of your Mission are generated by an exceptionally high number of apparently accidental meetings with traitors—and in such a short time, too. Correct?"

"More or less." I was recovering somewhat from the feeling that I had put myself in his hands. The empty eyes of the skull looked into mine; the smooth bone seemed to glow.

"Now you say the little old man was a traitor. Your own conclusion?"

"The captain who shot himself told me."

"He told you—then shot himself? Did you see the actual shooting?"

"Yes, that is . . . I heard a shot in the next room, then the thud of his falling body, and through a crack in the door I saw his leg, that is, a shoe . . ."

"Ah. And before that, the officer who was serving as your guide was arrested. Could you describe that arrest?"

"Two officers approached us, they took him aside and talked with him. I don't know what they said, I couldn't hear. Then the first officer took him away and the second went with me."

"Did anyone tell you that this was an arrest?"

"Well, no . . ."

"So you couldn't really swear to it?"

"I guess not, but the circumstances . . . particularly when you consider what happened later . . ."

"One thing at a time. You say the captain told you about the little old man, then you heard a shot, saw a shoe, and concluded that the captain himself was a traitor. As far as your guide is concerned, all you really know is that he was called away. Not much to go on, is it? Who's left? The spy in the bathroom—you found him asleep?"

"Yes."

"What would he be doing in a bathroom after photographing such vital documents? And taking a nap, too. The door wasn't locked, was it?"

"That's true, it wasn't."

"Are you still convinced that these were all traitors?"

I was silent.

"There, you see! Jumping to conclusions!"

"One moment," I interrupted. "Assuming they weren't traitors, how do you explain all of this? What was it, a play put on just for my benefit? But why? To what end?"

He smiled, all dimples, and said:

"Who knows? Perhaps they were inoculating you against treason by applying it in small doses. For that matter, even a man like Major Erms might do something you'd think suspicious, something a bit unusual—but surely you wouldn't take him for a traitor? Or would you?"

He watched me closely. How icily the eyes gleamed in that round and pleasant face . . .

He didn't wait for an answer.

"There remains one more nut for us to crack, the hardest: your instructions. They were in code, naturally. Were you able to take a good look at them? Are you absolutely sure they were a written account of your every movement and thought in the Building?"

"Well, no . . ." I replied reluctantly. "There was only time to read a paragraph or two. It had something about my going from office to office and people ignoring me, then about how vast and impersonal the Building was—operating in a random way—I can't recall the exact words, but I know they were practically taken out of my mouth . . ."

"That was all you managed to read?"

"Yes. Also, from time to time, people I meet make allusions to my experiences in the Building, even my very thoughts. Prandtl, for example. I told you about him."

"All he did was give you a sample of code, a demonstration."

"It seemed that way at first. But the sample happened to answer the question in my mind."

"Are you aware that superstitious people, when they find themselves in a critical period of their lives, often open the Bible at random to get some indication, some sign on which to predicate their future actions?"

"Yes, I've heard of that."

"You don't think it could be of real help?"

"Certainly not, it's a matter of pure luck which passage you open to."

"And your case, couldn't that be pure luck too, an accident?"

"There have been too many accidents," I said.

He didn't believe me. The mere facts I could give him; but the diabolical aura that surrounded them, that I was unable to convey. The doctor beamed.

"What you've told me," he said, "is no illusion or hallucination, I'm sure. But you do jump to conclusions. You are in such a terrible hurry to understand everything at once, to anticipate. I imagine they wish to develop certain qualities in you: an alert mind, the capacity for objective observation, attention to detail, the ability to distinguish the important from the unimportant, and many, many other things that will be indispensable in your work. I would say then that this was not, as you called it, a test, but rather a period of training; and training, when intensive, may sometimes bring one to the point of exhaustion, which is exactly what happened in your case."

I gazed into the empty eyes of the skull, no longer caring.

"But do forgive us about your clothes," said the doctor, beaming too much. "The nurse should be bringing them in any minute now . . ."

He kept talking. A thought occurred to me, vague, difficult to put into words . . .

"Do you have a section around here for—the mentally ill?" I asked. He blinked.

"Certainly we do," he replied kindly. "It's a regular

ward, but with just a few beds. Does that interest you? Who was it that said the spirit of an age speaks through its madness? An exaggeration, I'm sure. But if you'd like to see our ward, conduct your own observations firsthand, I have no objections. You'll be here for a while anyway."

"What?!"

"It would be advisable. But please understand, we are by no means holding you here."

"So you think that I . . ." I began calmly. He shuddered. The dimples vanished.

"Heavens, no! Nothing of the kind! You're simply over-worked, that's all. To prove it, I'm prepared to conduct you *ad altarem mente captorum*. Though actually we have only a few patients at the moment, all rather ordinary cases —*catatonia provocativa,* some residual obsessions, nervous ticks, compulsive winking and the like, collaboration dis-sociation, top priority hysteria, all according to textbook, quite boring really." Now he was warming up. "Recently, however, we acquired a fairly interesting case—a three-personality syndrome, tripsychoma, *folie en trois, Dreiei-niger Wahnsinn,* as it's variously called. Two personalities continually unmask one another, and the third gnaws at his arms and legs to keep from taking sides. Actually, it's nothing but *reservatio mentalis* with a few complications. You might also be interested in a condition called *mania autopersecutoria,* that is, a self-interrogation fit: the patient cross-examines himself—mutually, mind you—for up to forty hours without stopping, until he drops. Finally, we have a curious little item, autocryptic withdrawal."

"Oh?" I said, indifferent.

"The patient hides himself in his own body," the doctor explained, his face flushed with excitement. "He com-presses his identity to such a degree that he thinks, for example he's the malleus—you know, that little hammer-shaped bone in the middle ear—and that all the other parts of the body are enemy agents out to get him. At the moment, unfortunately, I can't take you on a tour of our ward; I have rounds to make elsewhere. Wait here, the nurse will bring your clothes. In the meantime you're welcome to look at my library. All I ask is that you try to relax—please!"

I was standing near the chair, feeling awkward in a bathrobe several sizes too large. The doctor shook my hand with his warm, plump hand and said:

"Chin up. Fewer suspicions, more simple courage, and everything will be fine, you'll see."

"Thanks," I mumbled.

At the door he smiled again, waved, and left. I stood around for a while, waiting for the nurse and my clothes, then went back to the table and took a good look at the skull. It grinned at me with a full set of big white teeth. Curious, I picked it up and snapped the jaw a few times— it was on a spring. There were hinges on the sides, the temples; the whole top came off like a lid. That is, could come off—I didn't care to open it, I liked the skull as it was, spherical. I admired the shine.

How elegantly the parietal bones fitted into the frontal, how smoothly the jagged edges interlocked! The occipital, on the other hand, was an enchanting moonscape with its many articulations and indentations, mounds, peaks, ravines, and that mighty crater, the foramen magnum, the gate for the spinal column. Ah, and where was the spine now? I sat, my elbows on the table, and meditated on skulls. Still no nurse.

I thought about various things. For instance, I knew a man once who suffered from a skeleton complex (his own), or rather a skeleton phobia, since it terrified him so much that he never spoke of it and even avoided touching himself in order not to feel beneath that soft envelope of flesh the hardness which waited to be free . . . I thought about how the skull was a symbol of death for us, a warning on a bottle of poison. Centuries ago the skeletons in anatomical atlases were not depicted in such stiff poses of warning, but were shown in attitudes of life: some danced, some leaned, their tibiae casually crossed, on sarcophagi while they directed their keen albeit funereal eye sockets straight at the reader. I even recalled a woodcut of two skeletons a-courting—and one of them was plainly bashful!

But here was a contemporary skull: clean, hygienic, scrubbed, the balustrades of the cheekbones nice and sleek, making little balconies beneath each orbital cavity— the nasal hole was a bit unpleasant, but then, who is without some minor blemish? And the smile! The smile made one stop and think. I lifted the skull, weighed it in my hand, rapped it with a knuckle, then—quickly—bent over and sniffed. Only dust, harmless, everyday dust tickling the nostrils, but then a whiff, a trace of something, something . . . until my nose touched the cold surface and I inhaled— yes—a faint, the faintest stink—another sniff—oh, foul play! Corruption!!

The reek betrayed the crime within. Like a drunkard, I breathed in the bloodiest, the most hideous murders behind that ivory elegance. I sniffed again: the gleam, the polish, the whiteness—all a vile hoax. Sickening! Horrible! I sniffed again, greedily, in terror, then hurled it on the table and frantically wiped my face, my hands, with the corner of my robe. But something drew me to it still . . . how it drew me . . .

The nurse entered with my suit carefully brushed and pressed. It looked like new. She placed it on the table by the skull, nodded stiffly, and left.

11

I dressed in an adjoining bathroom, leaving the door ajar so I could keep an eye on the skull. "My baleful beauty!" I thought. "What sweet revulsion to stare at you like this! How you thrill and chill me!" But it wasn't the skull I feared, I feared myself. What was drawing me to it, that well-boiled chunk of bone? What made it so attractive, what enticed me to sniff, sniff in a frenzy of disgust? The death that necessarily produced the skull? No, that death had no connection with this posthumous paperweight—nor with me, for that matter. I could understand, at least, why in the old days, long ago, they drank their wine from skull-caps. It added spice. I was thinking in this vein when suddenly a door squeaked open and someone entered the doctor's office. I closed my door to a crack and cautiously peeked out.

There were two of them, in bright pajamas. One had red hair, unevenly red, as if dyed and fading in spots. He was bending over and trying to read the titles of the doctor's books. The other was on the heavy side and had eyelids the color of strong tea; he sat at the table with the skull and said:

"Come on, you should have it down by now."

I adjusted my tie and walked in. The one who was sitting hardly looked at me. His neck was oddly white and flabby under that sunburnt, weather-beaten face.

"Want to play?" he asked, taking out a small tumbler from the pocket of his fuchsia pajamas, unscrewing it, rolling the dice out on the table.

"What do we play for?" I asked, hesitant.

"The stars, of course. Highest number wins, winner names the stakes."

He was already shaking the dice, rattling the bones.

136

I said nothing. He threw them and counted: eleven.

"Your turn."

He handed me the tumbler. I shook it and rolled two deuces and a four.

"I win!" he shouted. "Okay . . . this time, Mallinflor. He's a good one."

This time he threw thirteen.

"Five short," he said with a grin. I threw two fives and a six.

"Hell," he said. "All right, you name it."

"I don't know . . ." I muttered.

"Go on, don't be bashful!"

"The Admiral."

"You aim high!"

He threw seven. It was my turn again—two fives, but the third die rolled off the table and fell at the feet of the one who was looking at the books, his back to us.

"What is it, Cremator?" asked my partner, not getting up.

"A six," the other answered.

"What luck!" smiled my partner, displaying a set of rotten teeth. "Well?"

"A star," I began.

"Hell, for sixteen you can name a constellation!"

"A constellation? The Gold Spectacles," I said on impulse.

He blinked, he squinted at me—and the other came up and said:

"No sense playing any more, the doctor's here."

He had a slight stutter, and the face of an old squirrel: buckteeth, pointed whiskers and tiny, dull eyes surrounded by wrinkles.

"We haven't been introduced," he said. "I'm Sempriaq, the Senior Cremator. Sempriaq with a *q*." I mumbled my name and we shook hands.

The other asked:

"So where's the doctor?"

And he gave the dice a rattle.

"He'll be along. And you, you're an ambulatory?"

"I suppose," I said.

"We too. Came straight from work, saves time that way, quite a convenience. You don't happen to have a mirror, do you?"

"Stop it," said the doctor. Sempriaq ignored him.

"I should have one somewhere." I searched my pockets, then handed him a small, square mirror, scratched up quite a bit from long use. He looked himself over carefully and made a series of faces, as if trying to decide which was ugliest.

"Excellent!" he said. "It's been years since I looked so old!"

"And you're glad of it?" I asked.

"Oh yes. Even if I never see him again, this way at least—"

"See whom?"

"But you don't know, of course. It's my brother, my twin brother. He's on a Mission, so I may never see him again. This way at least—he did me dirt, you see—I can follow his misfortune."

"Stop it," said the other, clearly annoyed.

I studied them both. Sempriaq, though fairly thin and with a sunken chest, bore a striking resemblance to his heavy companion—in fact, they were as alike as two suits of slightly different cut but in exactly the same stage of wear, or as two clerks grown old together at adjacent desks. What had dried up and wrinkled over in one, sagged and folded in the other. Sempriaq, however, tried to preserve a certain style: every now and then he would smooth his mustache with a finger, or reach to adjust his collar—which wasn't there, since now he had on pajamas, chartreuse and silver.

"So you're going for treatments too?" he said, trying to resume our conversation.

"Another game?" the other asked with a nasal twang.

"Not the bones again?" Sempriaq sneered. "Can't you think up something else?"

An eye peered into the room through the keyhole, then vanished.

"There's Dolt," grumbled the other. "Up to his old tricks."

The door opened and a man in puce pajamas sauntered in, his clothes folded over one arm and the other holding a briefcase and a thermos. He was tall, painfully thin, his nose and Adam's apple jutted out like bent knives, and his eyes were pale and vacant, a peculiar contrast to his lively manner—particularly when he threw his head back and cried:

"Greetings, greetings, comrades and accomplices! When the doctor's called away, the patients will play!"

"What, another attack?" the heavy one asked calmly.

"Who can say? Brain failure, I suspect. Ha! But why wait, gentlemen? There is much merry to make!"

"Same old Dolt," sighed the heavy one, getting up. "One drunken orgy after another." Sempriaq touched his mustache pensively.

"Just us?"

"Just us! And a recruit to fill the cup. An able lad! Come, brave hearts, let us be off!"

I tried to slip away unnoticed. But just then he turned his watery eyes to me.

"What's this? A new man?" he said with exaggerated warmth. "We'd love to have you! A shot, a little harmless cheer, good for what ails you—ha! You must join us!"

I started to excuse myself, but was already arm in arm with the fuchsia pajamas and the puce pajamas, marching out the door, still protesting, and down the narrow corridor —the chartreuse pajamas went ahead and slammed the doors left and right along the way, and the slamming echoed up and down the entire level, announcing our mad progress. One door bounced back open, revealing a large room full of old women in shawls and high-buttoned shoes. Their voices blended into one complaining and quarrelsome sound as we passed.

"What was that?" I asked.

"Busybodies," said the cremator. "We keep them in reserve. This way, please." And he pushed me forward. I got a good whiff of his cheap hair tonic, and the smells of ink and soap.

The heavy one became strangely animated, began to bounce along, waving his arms and whistling—until, at the last door, he stopped and adjusted his pajamas with great ceremony, cleared his throat with even greater ceremony, and threw the door open.

"Welcome, welcome to our humble abode!"

The walls were bare; there was a huge, old-fashioned cupboard in the corner; and a banquet table stood in the middle of the room, its snow-white cloth covered with gleaming bottles and endless platters of food. In the far corner a young man with flowing hair—also in pajamas—was struggling with a stack of folding chairs, the kind one sees in outdoor cafés. He was opening and testing them, and raising a terrible racket in the process. The heavy one went to give him a hand, and the tall, emaciated organizer of this odd celebration, the one they called Dolt, folded his arms across his chest like a general on a hilltop, and surveyed the richly laden table as if it were tomorrow's battlefield.

"Excuse me," said a voice behind me, and I made way for the smiling young man, who was carrying several bottles of wine. He put them down and introduced himself.

"Klappershlang," he said, shaking my hand and blushing. "A trainee, as of yesterday . . ."

He couldn't have been more than twenty. His thick black hair curled around the pale forehead and fell to the ears in pretty ringlets.

"Comrades and accomplices, take your seats!" Dolt announced, rubbing his hands together.

We hardly had time to settle ourselves in those terribly rickety chairs when he filled our glasses and raised his own with a greedy, lopsided smile, and yelled:

"Gentlemen! The Building!"

"The Building!" we roared in one voice, clicked our glasses and drank. Whatever it was, it started a slow fire inside. Dolt refilled our glasses, licked his lips, made another toast, louder than the first, and emptied his glass in one swallow. The cremator sprawled in his chair, stuffed himself with hors d'oeuvres and with considerable finesse spit olive pits in the young man's direction. Dolt refilled and refilled. It was growing hot, and though the alcohol didn't seem to affect me, everything began to merge into a thick, shimmering liquid. The second the glasses were filled, they had to be emptied—as if there was some great urgency about it, as if they expected someone to rush in and call a halt to the proceedings. And their gaiety was unnaturally wild, for so few drinks.

"What kind of cake is this? Triple-layer?" asked the heavy one, his mouth full.

"No, triple-agent!" quipped Dolt, and the cremator laughed and broke into a volley of drunken jokes and off-color nursery rhymes.

"Your health, Dolt! And yours, you old necrophiliac!" roared the heavy one.

"Please, a thanatophile," said the cremator, reproachful.

Conversation became impossible; even shouts got lost in the confusion. There was toast after toast, down the hatch and bottoms up, and the jokes grew so awful that I had to drink to hide my disgust. Dolt sang in a piercing falsetto and performed an obscene dance with his fingers across the tablecloth while the cremator guzzled vodka and threw whole olives at the young man, who sat there in a stupor, and the heavy one bellowed like a bull:

"We're here because we're here!"

"Because we're here!"

"Because we're here!!" they howled in unison.

Then he jumped to his feet, tore off his wig and screamed, his bald head dripping sweat:

"Gentlemen! Hide and seek!"

"No, blindman's bluff!"

"No, charades!"

"Ho-ho! Ha-ha! Hee-hee!" they whinnied and brayed.

"Come fill the cup, and in the fire of Spring, your Winter-garment of Repentance fling!" cried the cremator, kissing the air.

"Gentlemen, I give you—I give you—I give you—gentlemen—the doctor!!" shrieked Dolt.

"And the ladies! Don't forget the ladies!"

"Oo-la-la!!"

"Hail, hail, the spies are hee-eere!" wailed the heavy one, then burped and looked around with a bleary eye, and yawned, revealing a pointed, delicate tongue, an almost feminine tongue.

What in heaven's name was I doing here among these loathsome lowlifes, participating in this revolting, pitiful binge of petty bureaucrats, this crude carousal of clerks? I was filled with horror.

"Gentlemen! I give you—our gatekeepers! Gentlemen—our cremators! I give you—" a voice piped from under the table.

"God save the King!"

"I'll drink to that!"

"Confusion to the enemy!"

"Prosit!"

"Long live the Archduke!"

"Skoal!" barked the chorus. I felt sorry for the young man; they were out to get him drunk, constantly filling his glass! The heavy one puffed up and turned purple, looked like he was ready to burst—only the flabby white neck didn't seem to match the rest of him. He had something to say, so he hurled a bottle to the floor to get everyone's attention, jumped up on a chair—but couldn't speak, gagged on his own laughter, waved his arms frantically for us to wait, then finally managed to shout:

"Riddles!!"

"Riddles! Riddles! Who's first?"

Dolt sang:

Clouds so dark, snow so white,
No moon up in the sky.
Hug me, kiss me, stay the night,
Oh, my darling spy! . . .

"Gentlemen! Here's number one! Who—who saw the instructions?"

A gale of laughter greeted the question. I shuddered as I watched the shaking bellies, the open mouths—the cremator grabbed the young man and they laughed until they cried. Again the glasses came together in a circle above the table and clinked. The cremator, like one possessed, imprinted passionate kisses upon the air, and Dolt gargled vodka—I noticed a little dent in his nose where the rim of the glass had hit it—another false nose. Not that I cared. The heavy one took off his pajama top and wiped his hairy armpits with it—the sweat trickled down his flabby body—and he unbuttoned his false ears.

"Oh, give me a peek and some secrets to leak," sang Dolt and the young man in harmony. "Where the spies and the counterspies play." The cremator joined in, off key:

"Where treason is heard an encouraging word—and there's plenty of men to betray!"

"Gentlemen! Riddle number two! What is marriage?" The heavy one shaked like a hairy woman. "Marriage is the smallest espionage unit," he said, but nobody was listening.

Red, screaming faces whirled around me. Was Dolt giving the cremator a sign by wiggling his ears? Impossible, they were both too drunk. Suddenly Sempriaq grabbed someone else's glass, gulped it down and smashed it on the floor. Then he stood up. Vodka and drool dribbled off his red whiskers.

"Gentlemen!" they yelled. "Pay attention! Look at that bearing, gentlemen! He needs a promotion!"

"Silence!" the cremator bawled, deathly pale. He reeled and clutched the table for support, cleared his throat, bared his squirrel-like teeth and broke into tears, crying:

"Alas, my youth! My sacred childhood! The haunts where I was wont to play! Whither have they fled? And wherefore? Where are the snows of yesteryear? Must all things piss away—that is, pass away?"

"Oh, shut up!" snapped Dolt. He looked the young man over very carefully, took out another full bottle and hissed:

"Don't you listen to him!"

And he put the bottle to the young man's lips and pulled back the head, forcing him to drink.

The gurgle of the emptying bottle was the only sound in the room. The cremator squinted, cleared his throat and continued:

"Am I not my left hand's keeper? Forty days and nights? My neighbor's ass, and much cattle? Behold, I stand before you, violated by existence . . ."

He stopped.

The young man fell limp into Dolt's arms. Dolt removed the empty bottle and said in a perfectly sober voice:

"That'll do."

"H'm," the heavy one grunted, bending over the young man and pushing the eyelids back with a thumb. Evidently satisfied, he let the body drop. It fell with a thud and rolled under the table, where it was soon snoring away.

The cremator took a seat, mopped his brow with a handkerchief, adjusted his mustache, and the others too began to stir themselves . . .

I couldn't believe my eyes. Everything was coming off: noses, eyebrows, wrinkles, birthmarks, they were all placed neatly on saucers. Stranger yet, the eyes cleared, the expressions grew more intelligent, the faces lost that dissipated office look. The tall, emaciated one (though actually, his cheeks were already filling out) pulled up a chair, gave a worldly smile, and said:

"Do forgive us this masquerade. An extremely unpleasant business, to be sure—yet quite unavoidable. *Force majeure.* Believe me when I tell you that it doesn't come easily to us. If a man imitates a pig, some of the piggishness is bound to rub off on him."

"Then he can unpig himself afterwards!" the cremator retorted from across the table, looking at his own hands with distaste.

I was speechless.

The tall one (he was shorter now) leaned against my chair. The cuff of an elegant dress shirt showed from under his pajama sleeve.

"The mire and the spire," he mused, "the eternal rhythm of history, the pendulum above the abyss . . ."

He raised his head.

"Now you can be our guest in earnest, though I fear our company might prove a bit too academic for your liking . . . We do tend to get abstruse at times . . ."

"What?" I blurted, not yet over this incredible transformation.

"Well, you know, we're all professors here. That's Professor Deluge," he pointed to the heavy one, who was dragging the young man out from under the table and trying, with difficulty, to prop him up against the wall. The trainee was apparently a high-ranking officer, to judge from the uniform that now showed under his pajamas.

"Deluge holds a chair in Scoposcopy."

"Scoposcopy?"

"Also, he's an accomplished cabalist and countercollaborationist. It was Deluge who doctored half the stars in the Galaxy."

"Dolt! That's a military secret!" cried the heavy professor in mock dismay. He straightened his clothes, reached for a glass of water and sprinkled some on his bald head.

"A secret? Now?" grinned Dolt.

"You're sure he's unconscious?" asked the cremator, his face in his hands, apparently fighting the effects of the alcohol he'd consumed.

"That's right, he snores too loud for such a young man," I said, realizing only now that all along they had been out to drink the young officer (disguised as a trainee) under the table.

"Young man? Why, he's old enough to be your father,"

snorted the heavy professor as he patted his bald head dry.

"You can believe Deluge, he's an old hand at this," Dolt reassured me—and lifted a corner of the tablecloth to let me see that the scholar in question discontinued below the waist.

"Dummy legs," he explained. "Hollow, of course. On occasions like these, eminently practical . . ."

"So you're all . . . professors?" I mumbled, unfortunately not completely sober.

"With the possible exception of our colleague the cremator. But then, his discipline is interdepartmental," said Dolt. "As director of our cadaveristics program and custodian—*custodia eius cremationi similis*—he holds a seat in the Faculty Senate."

"Then Mr. Sempriaq really is a cremator? I thought—"

"A cover? No. But you seem to be catching on. Yes," he said, nodding in the direction of the snoring, "it's hard work to lull suspicions."

"You shouldn't complain," said the heavy professor. "We didn't do at all badly this time. Often one has to stay up all night spinning yarns of bygone spies, plots of yore, operatives of old when finks were bold, and so forth and so on, then all about ultraspies and infrareds, the latest gadgets and gags, caches and tags—you talk yourself blue in the face before they're properly stupefied. And in winter, there's a log crackling on the fire and we sit around and sing coded carols, and there's always a draft—and I always catch a cold."

He sighed.

"Ah, yes," said the cremator, and he sang with squirrel-like sarcasm:

"Deck the halls with mikes and wiretaps, fa-la-la-la-la, la-la-la-la!"

"No more, Gatekeeper. I can't stand it!" cried Professor Deluge, shuddering.

"Gatekeeper?" I asked.

"You are surprised we call him Gatekeeper?" said Dolt.

"Professors we may be, but we have our nicknames too, our collegiate monikers . . . Deluge here was christened 'Proteus' by his fraternity. 'Gatekeeper' . . . well, in the sense that he guards the gate to the Building, the door with only one side, the side facing us . . ."

That was unclear, but I didn't dare question him further. So to ask something, I asked:

"And what is your field, Professor?"

"Nanosemy, and I teach a seminar on pseudosemeiology. Also, I dabble in decerebration and defecation—trepans and bedpans, you know—just a hobby."

"Such modesty," said Professor Deluge. "I'll have you know that our Professor Dolt is the world's greatest authority on blackmail, and that his work, *The Anatomy of Treason,* is an absolute must for anyone planning to betray his country. But enough of this, talking makes the throat dry—*nunc est bibendum!*"

And he uncorked a bottle.

"You mean," I said, thoroughly confused, "we're going to drink again?"

"Good Lord man, why else are we here?"

"But . . . we've already had so much . . ."

"*That* drinking doesn't count, it was only for appearances," the heavy professor patiently explained. "Anyhow, we're not drinking cheap vodka and raw wine, but the best cognac, brandy, all vintage stuff."

"Well, I suppose . . ."

The bottle made its way around the table; its noble contents, ceremoniously sniffed and sipped, soon restored us, lifted our spirits, softened the memory of our recent trials. From the ensuing conversation I learned that Professor Dolt had more than a passing interest in Ancient Greece.

"A change of pace?" I inquired.

"Whatever do you mean? Why, the Trojan Horse marked the birth of cryptoequestrianism! And think of the unmasking of Circe by Odysseus! Or the musical sabotage of the sirens! And the omens, the riddles, the oracles—or take Zeus's infiltration in the guise of a swan!"

"Apropos," Sempriaq interrupted, "do you know the opera *Cadaveria Rusticana?*"

"Hellenic studies, a veritable gold mine!" Dolt continued, ignoring the cremator.

"Undoubtedly," I agreed. "But . . . may I ask, Professor, exactly what the field you mentioned—Nanosemy, was it? —what it deals with? . . ."

"Of course you may. Nanosemy, yes. Consider first: what is our earthly existence but a neverending culling of intelligence? We seek to discover Nature's secrets. In Rome they had but one name for the scholar-explorer and the scout-agent: *speculator.* And indeed, the scientist is a spy *par excellence* and, for that matter, *par force.* He is Humanity's Plant in the Great Lap of Existence!"

He filled my glass.

"Yes, spying is man's *qualitas occulta,* and has been from earliest times. In the Middle Ages we have spyeries, espyals . . . To spy, *spionieren, spitzeln, espionner, skopiaō, szpiegować, špijunirati* . . . Treason, *tresun, treysoun, tradere, trahison* . . . Mata Hari, Dreyfus, Delilah, Wallenstein . . . *Verily I say unto you, that one of you shall betray me.—Machinations, hollowness, treachery, and all ruinous disorders.—A treason and a stratagem.—I come no Spie with purpose to explore the secrets of your Realm.— We come not single spies, but in battalions.—This blessed plot* . . . But I digress . . . Where were we? My field, yes. What does it mean? Meaning. And so we enter the realm of semantics. One must tread carefully here! Consider: from earliest times man did little else but assign meanings—to the stones, the skulls, the sun, other people, and the meanings required that he create theories—life after death, totems, cults, all sorts of myths and legends, black bile and yellow bile, love of God and country, being and nothingness —and so it went, the meanings shaped and regulated human life, became its substance, its frame and foundation— but also a fatal limitation and a trap! The meanings, you see, grew obsolete in time, were eventually lost, yet how could the following generations discard their heritage, particularly when so many of their worthy ancestors had been crucified for those nonexistent gods, or had labored so long and mightily over the philosopher's stone, phlogiston, ectoplasm, the ether? It was considered that this layering of new meanings upon old was a natural, organic process, a semantic evolution—yet observe how a phrase like 'great discovery' is bled of sense, devalued, made common coin, until now we give it freely to the latest model of bomb . . . But do have some more cognac."

And he filled my glass.

"And so," continued Dolt with a thoughtful smile, adjusting his nose. "Where does this lead us? Demisemiotics! It's quite simple, really, the taking away of meaning . . ."

"Oh?" I said, then bit my lip, ashamed of my own ignorance. He took no notice.

"Yes, meaning must be disposed of!" he said heatedly. "History has crippled us long enough with its endless explanations, ratiocinations, mystifications! In my work, we do not simply falsify atoms and doctor the stars—we proceed very slowly, methodically, with the utmost care, to deprive everything, absolutely everything, of its meaning."

"But isn't that really—a kind of destruction?"

He gave me a sharp look. The others whispered and fell silent. The old officer propped up against the wall continued to snore.

"An interesting observation. Destruction, you say? Consider: when you create something, anything, a rocket or a new fork, there are always so many problems, doubts, complications! But if you destroy (let's use that inaccurate term for the sake of argument), whatever else one may say about it, it is unquestionably clean and simple."

"So you advocate destruction?" I asked, unable to suppress an idiotic grin.

"Must be the cognac," he said, refilling my glass with a smile. We drank.

"Besides, we aren't even here," he added.

"How do you mean?"

"Have you any idea of the mathematical probabilities involved for any given chunk of matter in the universe to be eligible for participation in the biosphere, whether as a leaf, a sausage, or even drinkable water? Or breathable air? The odds are about a quadrillion to one against it! Our universe is a prodigiously lifeless place. One particle in a quadrillion may enter into the life cycle, the procession of birth and death, growth and decay—consider what a rare event that must be. And now I ask you to consider not the probability of a piece of food, or of a drop of water, or of a breath of air—but the probability of an embryo! Take the ratio of the mass of the universe—the burnt-out suns, the frozen planets, those cosmic garbage dumps we call nebulae, that enormous cloaca of dust and rubble and noxious gas we think of as the Milky Way, all that thermonuclear fermentation, that swirling of debris—take the ratio of that total mass to the mass of a human body; there you have your probability for a chunk of matter, equal in weight to a man, to *be* a man—and that probability is negligible!"

"Negligible?" I said.

"In other words, you and I, all of us in this room, statistically we can't exist, we aren't really here . . ."

"What?" I blinked, trying to clear my vision.

"We aren't here," repeated Dolt, and burst out laughing with the others.

It was a joke, of course, one of those clever scientific jokes. It didn't strike me as particularly funny, but I laughed to be polite.

The empty bottles disappeared and full ones took their place.

I was attentive as the scholars conversed, but understood less and less. I had had too much to drink. Someone, possibly the cremator, held forth on the death agony as a test of strength. Professor Deluge engaged Professor Dolt in a debate on dementogeny and psychophagia—or something like that—then they talked of recent breakthroughs, the *Machina Mistificatrix,* and my head kept nodding no matter how hard I tried to sit up straight, and the voices seemed to come from a great distance.

"Is he ready?" someone asked. I tried to see who it was, but everything kept revolving—was I really that drunk?—and then I found I couldn't even think, someone was doing it for me. I floated in a cloud of tiny sparks, latched onto the table and laid my burning face on it, like a dog.

Before me was the slender stem of a wineglass, the dainty leg of an elegant goblet, a delicate crystal thigh ... I told her I would always be true, I wept in gratitude, and overhead they drank and held forth—truly, those caps and gowns did hold their liquor well!

Then there was nothing, and when I came to, my throbbing head still rested on the table. There were crumbs on my nose. I heard voices.

"The universe, I betrayed the universe ... *mea culpa,* I confess it ...."

"All right, that's enough."

"Those were my orders, my orders ...."

"Come on, have a glass of water."

"Is he asleep?" someone asked.

"Don't worry, he's out cold."

But there was dead silence when I stirred and opened my eyes. Nothing had changed. The old officer was still snoring away in a corner. Bottles and faces swam before my eyes.

"*Silentium,* gentlemen!"

"*Gaudeamus Isidor!*"

"*Nunc est Gaudium atque Bibendum!*" came a cry from far away.

"There's no difference," I thought. "It's the same as before, except in Latin."

"Gentlemen!" shouted Dolt. "*Suaviter in re, fortiter in modo ... Spectator debet esse elegans, penetrans et bidexter ... Vivant omnes virgines,* gentlemen! *Vive la Maison!* Cheers!"

Everything whirled around, red things, sweaty things, white things, heavy things. . . Where before they had chortled, "The ladies! Oo-la-la!" now it was *Frivolitas in duo corpore, Venus Invigilatrix*," and more of the same. I tried to ask them why, but no one would listen to me. They jumped on their chairs, delivered speeches, sat down again, sang, danced in a circle. "We did that before!" I protested, but they laughed and pulled me along. "Toom-ba-toom-ba-toom-ba-ba!" boomed the heavy one, and we all joined hands and pranced and stamped our way into an enormous hall. A cold draft from somewhere sobered me up a little, and I looked around.

A kind of *Theatrum Anatomicum,* a lecture hall with rising tiers of chairs, and in the center a podium, lectern, blackboards, erasers, chalk, shelves of specimens preserved in alcohol, and on the table empty jars, waiting to be filled —so *this* was where the Commander in Chief got his supply! A gentleman in black approached our dancing group. The cremator ground to a halt and blew out air like an old locomotive; I uncoupled my car from the train and waited to see what would happen next.

"Ah! If it isn't Professor Schnuffel! Welcome, welcome, beloved colleague!" cried Deluge, and his greeting echoed and reechoed. The others also stopped their prancing to bow and shake his hand. The new professor looked quite venerable in his gray hair and tails.

"Professor Shuffle! Kindly enlighten us on this matter of bottom priority, to wit, what in the hell is it?" bellowed Dolt and, to accentuate his lack of respect, hopped on one leg.

"The brain, *membra dissecta,*" replied the old man in black. And indeed, there on the table were large, plaster sections of the human brain, all carefully mounted and labeled, resembling marble viscera, or perhaps a modern sculptor's madness. The professor brushed one with a feather duster.

"The brain?!" Dolt shrieked with glee. "Gentlemen! I give you our pride and joy—the brain!" He lifted his glass. "A toast that is bacchic, bucolic, and anacoluthic!"

He filled our glasses, then turned and read the labels like a litany:

"O, *gyrus fornicatus!*" he intoned, and the others took up the chorus, howling with laughter.

"O, *tuber cinerum! O, striatum! O, corpora quadrigemina,* four rounded bodies!"

"Rounded bodies!" they roared with delight. The old man in the tuxedo continued his dusting as if nothing had happened.

"O, *sella turcica! Chiasma opticum!* Mammillary body!" chanted Dolt.

"Mammillary body!" yelled the cremator.

"O, *hippocampus! Pons Varolii! O,* fissure of Rolando!"

"*Dura mater, pia mater, alma mater!* And gentlemen, let us not forget *mater hari!*"

"Careful, there's formaldehyde," cautioned Professor Schnuffel or Shuffle.

"Formol—formalin—formaldehyde!"

They joined hands and dragged the venerable anatomy professor with them, making him their leader and waving his feather duster about like a banner. I sat in one of the chairs and watched, trying to bring things into focus. Drunken shouts and stamping feet boomed and echoed in the dark, and the domed ceiling looked down on us like a monstrous eye.

On a metal stand next to me was a skeleton, stooped and toothless, in an attitude of somber resignation. The left hand was short one finger—I gasped, I looked closer. Something glittered, dangling from a rib ... gold spectacles ...

Was this, then, his final destination? A display for medical students? And was this to be our third, our final meeting? And was it all to end like this? ...

"Catch, Gatekeeper!" cried Dolt. "*Haec locus, ubi Troia fuit!* Professor Shrapnel! I bestow upon you the Order of the Garter Snake, *Denuntiatio Constructiva,* the Distinguished Noose of Honor!"

"Watch out!" hissed the gray anatomist as they recklessly pulled him along, his tails flapping wildly. The warning came too late—they crashed into the shelves and brought everything down, the jars shattered on the floor, the alcohol spilled out and, with it, the matted freaks within...

The stench of corruption, bottled up for so many years, now billowed out and filled the auditorium. The revelers fled, leaving the old man to his despair, and I followed them back to our room and slammed the door.

More bottles, corks popping, and an endless pouring and roaring, so I hid in an armchair and gratefully went out with the tide, wondering only how one could put on gold spectacles if there were no ears left. Overcome with grief, I sank beneath the waves...

Suddenly an apparition got in my way, pale, dripping sweat, unusually long.

"What a long face you have, Professor," I said, enunciating each syllable with care.

The table made a good pillow. But Dolt smiled a wicked, left-handed smile and whispered:

"Only a worm can play the worm..."

"What a long face," I whispered in alarm.

"Never mind the face. You know what I am?"

"Certainly... Professor Dolt, sabotage..."

"No, that's Deluge... My mission is to—neutralize—Him."

I tried to sit up but couldn't.

"What?"

"*He* must be put out of action."

"Deluge?"

"Not Deluge—Him, you know, the One who—rested on the seventh day." And the left side smiled again. The right remained sad.

"You're joking."

"Not at all. We've checked... up there, in the heavens above... we have our sources of information, you know."

"Of course," I muttered. "Professor?"

"Yes?"

"Tell me, what's a triple?"

He gave me a hug and breathed alcohol in my face.

"I'll tell you. You're young, but you're one of us, and I'm one of us, so I'll tell you. Everything. Now, say someone's one of us . . . but he's also—you know—you can tell, right?"

"He's not—one of us," I said.

"Right! You can tell! But sometimes—you can't tell. You think someone's one of us, but *they* got to him and then he wasn't any more—and then *we* got to him, and he was—but he still has to look like he isn't, that is, like he only *looks* like he is! But they get wise to him and—now he isn't again, but he has to *look* like he isn't—or *we'll* get wise —and that's a triple!"

"Of course," I replied. "And a quadruple's the same, only more."

"Exactly! Now if you like, I'll swear you in."

"You?"

"Me."

"But you're a professor!"

"So? I also swear in agents."

"For which side?"

"You really want to know?"

"Well . . ."

"You're not so dumb as you look. You'll go far." He chucked me under the chin like a fond father. How very old he looked! And so suddenly!

"And you're not even ticklish," he said with an approving wink. "Now tell me, what's galactoplexia?"

"Galactoplexia?"

"Give up? The end of the world! Ha!"

Could it be that under the influence of alcohol, the crude office-clerk element was winning out over the professorial? My head ached at the thought. Dolt stared at me with his icicle eyes.

Somebody was scratching my leg. The cremator surfaced from under the tablecloth, climbed onto my knees and said:

"How sweet it is to hear old friends third-degree each other . . . like sniffing a rose in spring . . . exchanging innocent lies . . ."

He wrapped his arms around my neck and whispered:

"Friend. Long-lost brother. Name it, it's yours, whatever you want, I'll give you the world . . ."

"Professor, please!" I said, struggling with him. He hung on me like a sack of potatoes and tried to kiss me, pricking my cheeks with his stubby whiskers until they pulled him off and he staggered back—holding up a plate.

A plate? Wait! I racked my brains. Yes, there was something—plates! Someone mentioned plates! But who, and what did it mean?

There was a great commotion, a crowd of people jumped up and ran about: in the middle of the room sat the heavy professor, rocked by violent hiccups, a wet rag on his bald head. The hiccups made a curious counterpoint with the snoring from the corner.

"Scare him! Frighten him!"

We gathered in a circle around him. I swayed on rubber legs. He looked at us, confused, gesturing for help—he couldn't speak for the hiccups—the eyes bulged hideously, and the chair creaked beneath him, so powerful were the spasms.

"He's signaling!" hissed the cremator, listening closely and holding his plate high in the air. "Hear it?"

"No! N-o!" the heavy one protested, but his protest was lost in a veritable storm of hiccups.

"Signaling, eh?" Dolt said grimly and squeezed my hand.

"No, I swear!!"

"Count them!" roared the multitude.

We counted the hiccups in ominous chorus:

"Eleven, twelve, thirteen."

"Traitor!" hurled the cremator, and pointed an accusing finger.

The heavy one turned a deep purple, the sweat poured down his face, he trembled . . .

"Fourteen, fifteen . . ."

I waited, my fingers numb in Dolt's iron grip. The heavy one held his breath, bit his fist—but the hiccup came and knocked him off his chair.

"Six–"

He shuddered, coughed, then lay still. Finally the swollen eyelids flickered open and peace reigned once more on that flabby face.

"Thanks," he whispered. "Thanks."

And we returned to the table as if nothing had happened. I was still drunk, but in a different way: everything was free and easy, my movements, my speech, and the part of me that had always watched and stood guard—that part was gone now, and I greeted its disappearance with gay abandon.

Before I knew it, Dolt was lecturing me on the nature of the Building's nature. He sang this song:

> Hey, the Building, hey!
> What makes the Building stay?
> The Antibuilding makes it stay!
> Hey!

Then he spoke of sodomystics and gomorrhoids. I decided to ignore the plate which the cremator was waving at me from across the room.

"I see it!" I yelled in defiance. "It's a plate! But I'll do what I want! I don't care! I'm free as a bird!"

"Free as a bird!" said Dolt, patting my knee with a left-handed laugh. He inquired into my experiences as a spy, asked how the Building was treating me, and so on. I talked.

"And what happened then?" he asked, showing interest.

I told him everything—in the strictest confidence, since I still wasn't sure of the others. The priest, Dolt said, was an abbé provocateur; and of the little old man in the gold spectacles he had this to say:

"Serves him right. He completely lost his head in the coffin sequence."

Sempriaq left the table and went to talk something over with the heavy one, who still sat in the middle of the room and was pouring water on his head.

"A possible conspiracy," I said to Dolt, pointing them out.

"Pish tush," he said. "Let's get back to you. What did the doctor say?"

When he heard the rest of my story, he sighed, solemnly shook my hand, and said:

"You are distraught. But you needn't be, you needn't be . . . Look at me: roaring drunk. Positively. Sober, it's a different story, but now—my heart is open to you. You're one of us, I'm one of us . . . Do you know what I am? You don't know what I am."

"You told me, you—"

"I didn't tell you. Now I'll tell you. Yes. Plenipotentiary of Transcendental Affairs. But that's nothing. Now I'll tell you the truth: *la Maison c'est moi*. I am the Building. Triples, quadruples, quintuples—that's nothing, mere child's play. Hide-and-seek. Now here's the Building. And here's the Antibuilding. Two colossi. Since the world began. And everyone, you understand, has been approached by now. The Building consists entirely of enemy agents; the Antibuilding is ours, down to the last man!"

"Of course," I said, trying desperately not to believe this unbelievable revelation.

"Everyone's a plant, infiltration is complete, complete and mutual—ours pretend to be ours, theirs theirs—so everything remains the same!"

"The same?"

"The Building stands firm by virtue of the fact that ours became theirs over a span of many years, gradually, plant by plant, keeping the structure, the system intact. Everything was carefully preserved: ranks, promotions, decorations, unmaskings, regulations, security precautions, surveillance, office procedures and routines, seals and signatures, everything in triplicate—and so by the grace of Almighty Bureaucracy did the Building remain true to itself, keep the faith, and turn betrayal to unswerving loyalty!!"

"Amazing!" I exclaimed, all goose flesh.

"But true, my boy, but true. Consider that the business of entrapment, blackmail, planting an agent, requires the utmost security, absolute secrecy, otherwise you risk exposure and the game is up. Hence, only one of theirs *there* knows about a given one of theirs *here,* and vice versa. Also, since his superiors and subordinates think he's one of ours, he must report for work like everyone else, take and give orders, track down enemy agents in earnest and neutralize them. Thus he does the Building's work. And if in the line of duty he should happen to steal or photograph a few secret documents, no harm is done: the information goes *there,* to the Antibuilding, into the hands of *our* people."

"And vice versa?" I whispered, awed by the vision of treachery on such a scale.

"Yes, unfortunately. Clever of you to observe that."

"And the shooting in the hall? And the suicides?" My question must have hit a nerve—his face clouded over, his mouth gave a left-handed twitch.

"There are slip-ups now and then, leaks—and there are quotas to meet. The Building continues to recruit and swear in new agents—it dare not stop—and complications result. For example, a double might unmask a triple that's really a quadruple. The situation is hardly improved by the recent appearance of sextuples and septuples, overenthusiastic types . . ."

"And the spy in the bathroom, what about him?"

"Who knows? A free lance, perhaps, a maverick, a gentleman of the old school, an unreconstructed liberal, a dreamer, the kind that waits and hopes to seize the Document of documents, the Secret of secrets—single-handed. Idle fancies, since only the collective can achieve anything, and he knows this, and that is why he despairs . . ."

"Then what should *I* do?"

"Above all, get involved, take sides, don't slip into the pit of self-pity and escapist fantasies. It's the little individual, remember, that ends up caught between the Devil and the deep blue sea."

The cremator held up two plates. I waved him away.

"Could you be more specific?"

"Diversify, dig in, hold out, buy low, sell high, and to thine own self be true."

"I see. There's one other thing—how is it you know so much about the Building if everything is supposed to be so secret? After all, you said that—" But the cremator came up and interrupted me with his plates. "I'm not interested in your plates!" I cried, pushed him away, and turned to Dolt. "I mean, how do you know?"

"Know what?"

"You know, what you were just telling me."

"I know?"

"You know, how both camps infiltrated one another, mutually, to the last man, and how the Building was really the Antibuilding and vice versa, and treason wasn't treason, but loyalty . . . How did you find all this out?"

"How?" he said, inspecting his fingernails.

"I'm asking you!"

"Me?" He looked up and gave me an icy stare.

"Yes! How did you—?"

"How did I what?" The room was silent, too silent.

"You know . . . find all this out?"

"I don't know," he said with a sneer, "what you're talking about."

I turned pale, the words stuck in my throat—and I realized, suddenly, that the officer in the corner was no longer snoring, but getting up, stretching, removing his pajamas and straightening his uniform, then walking briskly up to us and saying:

"Are you prepared to testify that this employee, known under the name of Dolt *alias* Professor of Nanosemy and Demisemiotics *alias* The False Statistician *alias* Screw *alias*

Plauderton, did willfully slander and abuse the Building and did attempt by such slander and abuse to entice you to high treason, lèse maison, asubordination, nonprovocation, unsabotage and null espionage, and that the said Dolt did contrive to ensnare you thereby in his nefarious snares, schemes and coils?"

I looked around. The heavy one stroked his flabby neck. Dolt fixed his white, expressionless eyes on me. The cremator had turned his back to us and was examining his plates, as if refusing to acknowledge what was taking place.

"In the name of the Building I call you forth to bear testimony and witness against this man!" said the officer severely.

Numb, I shook my head. The officer stepped forward, seemed to trip, grabbed me to right himself—and whispered in my ear:

"Idiot! This is your Mission!"

Then he stepped back and said, in the same stern tone: "Speak! We are waiting!"

I looked to the others for help. They looked away. Dolt began to tremble.

"Yes," I mumbled.

"Yes, what?"

"Well, he said some things . . ."

"Treasonous things?"

"No!! I swear!" screamed Dolt.

"Silence!" The officer turned to me. "Go on."

"Well . . . he did say that treason . . . was loyalty . . ."

"Treason loyalty?!"

"In a sense . . . that is, we were talking in general . . ."

"Did he say it or not?!"

"He did," I whispered, and after a moment of silence they burst out laughing; the heavy one held his belly and bounced in his chair, Dolt wheezed, and the officer (young again) danced around the table and yelled:

"He did it! He ratted! He squealed! He sang!"

"Stool pigeon! Tattletale! Stool pigeon! Tattletale!" they crowed, doubled up with laughter.

Only the cremator remained aloof, watching the scene with a sardonic smile.

"Enough!" said Dolt, triumphant. "It's time for us to go."

The heavy one buttoned his collar; the young officer, weary but satisfied, rinsed his mouth out with seltzer. They completely ignored me. I was stunned, speechless. Dolt picked up his briefcase and thermos, threw his suit over his shoulder and strode out, arm in arm with the heavy one.

The cremator turned around at the door and pointed eloquently at the plates left on the table. This clearly meant: "I gave you the signs! You have only yourself to blame!"

Only the young man remained, and he was leaving. I stood in his way—he stopped—I clutched his arm.

"It was all a game, wasn't it? How could you!"

"Please, sir," he said, trying to free his arm, but evidently too embarrassed to look me in the eye. "That was the Onion."

"The Onion?"

"That's what it's called in the tactical nomenclature. Even our jokes are classified . . . code names . . ."

"That was a *joke?*"

"Don't be angry, sir. It was no picnic for me either to lie there and snore all that time. But you know, orders are orders . . ." And he shrugged.

"Just tell me—what was the point of it all?"

"It isn't all that simple, sir. I mean . . . in a way, it was just a joke, really, for you at least . . . The Professor might have wanted to watch the reactions—"

"My reactions?"

"No, Sempriaq's. Now if you'll excuse me, I have to be off. And really, there's nothing for you to worry about—you're in the clear."

He skipped out like a schoolboy, giving the cupboard a tap on his way.

I was alone with the remains of the party: overturned

chairs, leftovers, dirty plates, broken plates, crumbs, bottles, wine-stained tablecloth—a dismal scene. There was some-one knocking. But the room was empty. The knocking re-turned, more persistent. I listened closely. One, two, three, four taps. It sounded like wood—the cupboard!

The key was in the lock; I turned it and the door slid open by itself. Inside, hunched over, sat Father Orfini. He wore a cassock over his uniform and held a pile of papers on his knee. He didn't notice me at first, he was writing something. At last he finished, dotted an *i,* put a period, then stretched his legs, got off his little stool and stepped out of the cupboard, pale and serious.

12

"We need your signature on this," he said, placing the papers on the table.

"What is it?"

I had my hands up, as if to defend myself against some attack. The papers lay next to the cremator's plates, between two wine stains.

"For our records."

"Records? What is it, a confession? Or another joke?"

"It's merely the minutes of what transpired here, nothing more. Please sign."

"And if I refuse?" I said, easing myself into a chair. I had a splitting headache.

"It's only a formality."

"I won't sign."

"Very well."

He gathered up the papers, folded them, put them in a pocket of his uniform, buttoned up his cassock—and was a simple priest again. He looked at me, apparently waiting for something.

"You were sitting there the whole time, Father?" I asked, my face in my hands. All that liquor left me feeling dirty, befouled.

"I was."

"It must have been stuffy in there."

"Not at all," he replied calmly, "it's fully air-conditioned."

"Ah."

I was too tired even to bother saying what I thought of him. My left leg began to dance. I let it.

"Permit me to explain what happened," he said, standing above me. He waited for me to acknowledge this intention, but when I didn't respond (only the leg was shaking like some wound-up mechanism), he went on:

"That 'joke' was in reality the showdown between Dolt and Sempriaq. You were to decide the issue. The recruit was in Dolt's employ, and Deluge served as witness. Actually, the whole thing was staged by Dolt; all he needed was a suitable actor, someone to play it out to his advantage. He must have heard of you from the doctor. That's all I know."

"You're lying," I whispered through my hands.

"I'm lying," he echoed. "Dolt engineered this intrigue entirely on his own. But Deluge got wind of it and informed the Section. Thus, unbeknownst to Dolt, the intrigue had become official, that is, it was now a legitimate operation under the auspices of the Section. The Chief sent me to protocol the proceedings. Unfortunately, the situation has turned out to be much more complex than was anticipated. The recruit, you see, tapped the cupboard as he left, indicating that he was aware of my presence. No one else in the room was. Now, the Chief couldn't have ordered him to tap, since the recruit does not come under his jurisdiction. We must conclude, therefore, that the recruit was acting under orders from higher up. Thus, he was playing a double game, on one hand obedient to Dolt, his superior, and on the other hand in contact with someone superior to Dolt. But why was he told to tap? My orders were to record everything that took place, so I must include the tap in my report. The Chief will read the report and realize that disciplinary action should not be initiated against the recruit for his part in Dolt's intrigue, since the recruit demonstrated by betraying his awareness of my presence in the cupboard that he was acting under orders from higher up and was therefore not really an accomplice in Dolt's intrigue. To sum up, the action takes place on three levels: the showdown between Dolt and Sempriaq; the surveillance by the Section, through me, of Dolt, Sempriaq and the others, which was personally ordered by the Chief; and finally, the surveillance of our surveillance, through the recruit, by someone higher up, higher therefore than the Section—that means the Department.

"And that complicates things considerably. Why did the Department, rather than work directly with the Section, choose to operate in such a roundabout fashion, revealing its participation in the affair only by a tap on a cupboard? Here we must go back to Dolt. It is conceivable that what he presented to Sempriaq and Deluge as an independent action had in reality been cleared with the Department, and that the supposed intrigue was not to defeat Sempriaq in the debate over the value of Operation Onion, defeat him, that is, in an academic sense, but actually to destroy him, and destroy any of the other members of that 'party' who might break the fundamental rule of loyalty by *not* informing the authorities of his (Dolt's) intrigue. So the loyalty test presents a new side to the problem, a fourth level. And there is a fifth. You see, there had to be two denunciations: Professor Deluge's to the Section, and the recruit's to the Department (obviously, the Department could not have given him the order to tap on the cupboard without having been informed of the intrigue in the first place). Professor Deluge's denunciation is the more interesting, I think. Both the Department and the recruit acted according to regulations throughout. But Deluge—Deluge knew what he was doing. If he betrayed Dolt to the Section instead of to the Department, it was because he was so ordered. In other words, he was not really betraying Dolt; he was following instructions, earlier instructions—also from the Department. But what was the Department after? It already had two people on the case, Dolt and the recruit. Why a third? To see what the Section would do with an unsolicited denunciation? But the Section would have to forward even a nonregulation denunciation to the Department —which it in fact did, at the same time sending one of its own into the field, namely me. Either way, Deluge is definitely a Department plant. The only one who acted on his own in response to Dolt's challenge was therefore Sempriaq. Note, however, that he tried to warn you of the intrigue, to tell you that Dolt's words of advice, that all his confidences were only the lines of a cunning play, of an insidious plot, or—in other words—part of a play-plot, a *plate*. Now any attempt to influence your final decision, any signal or sign in whatever form was expressly forbidden according to the rules set down and agreed to by both parties. (Deluge described them in great detail in his denunciation.) By showing you the plate, therefore, Sempriaq clearly broke the rules. The question is, why? Simply to win? Hardly— that kind of victory would be declared invalid. Anyway, you were obviously blind to the import of his most ingenious signal. Then too, the cremator had nothing to gain in warning you, if by that very act he automatically disqualified himself. Still, he warned you. Why? Obviously to let Dolt know that he knew of Dolt's real intrigue with the Department and that he was well aware that the ostensible (first) intrigue was indeed ostensible. But such knowledge could only have been gained with the consent of those higher up . . . It becomes evident, then, that all present (except for myself, hidden in the cupboard) were working for the Department."

"Not me," I said.

"Ah, but you were! Your coffee was sweetened!"

"What?"

"The coffee they threw in your face, remember? The sugar in it made you sticky, and that necessitated a shower, which in turn enabled them to remove your clothes and accustom you to moving about in a bathrobe, and from a bathrobe to pajamas the transition is not so great . . . Besides, the doctor would never have dared to hand you over to Dolt—without orders. So you see, everyone, yourself included, was of the Department. Do you realize what that means?"

"No."

"If Sempriaq gave up his chance to win by showing you the plate, then there was really no contest. Moreover, if he and the other two, and yourself—if all of you were pawns on the same side, then there was no other side! The joke was not Dolt's then, but the Department's! But I see you don't believe me."

"I don't."

"Of course you don't, how could you? After all, why would a Department, and a powerful Department at that, waste its valuable time on practical jokes? Impossible! No, there must be some deeper meaning in all this . . . It was Dolt, remember, who wished to make you the butt of his joke, not the Department. The Department mocked everyone! An odd joke, you say? It all depends on the point of view. Usually, when we find something perfect in every respect but perfectly meaningless, we laugh. Yet if it's on a sufficiently large scale, we don't . . . Take the sun, for example, its prominences like hair in curlers, or a galaxy with all its wandering garbage—a grotesque carrousel, isn't it? And the metagalaxy with all that dandruff . . . Really, how can anyone take infinity seriously? Just look at that incredible jumble they call the zodiac! But have you ever seen a lampoon on a sun or a galaxy? Of course you haven't— we prefer not to make fun of such things. The joke, after all, might very well turn out to be on us . . . So we pretend not to notice the indiscriminate way the universe goes about its business; we say that it is what it is, namely everything, and surely *everything* can't be just a joke. Anything enormous, immense beyond belief or reckoning—has to be serious. Size, how we worship size! Believe me, if there were a turd big as a mountain, its summit hidden in the clouds, we would bend the knee and do it reverence. So I musn't insist that it was all a joke. You don't want it to be all a joke, do you? The thought that your suffering might be incidental and not intentional, that no one takes an interest in it, not even a sadistic interest, for the simple reason that it concerns not a soul but yourself—surely that's an unbearable thought. But Mystery offers a way out, a way out of all monstrous absurdities. With Mystery, one can at least hope . . . That's all I wanted to say. Except that I oversimplified when speaking of the Department. Many threads lead there, you see, but they do not end there. No, they travel further, they branch and spread throughout the Building. It was the Building's joke, in the final analysis. Or no one's—whatever you like . . . And now you know everything."

"I only know that you told me what they told you to tell me."

"And you wouldn't believe me if I denied that, and you shouldn't, because even if I did, it probably wouldn't be the truth. Who knows?"

"Don't you?"

"After what I've just said, you should know better than that. True, I was not actually given any such order. But perhaps my superior was, perhaps he chose that I should carry it out without my knowledge. Or perhaps the choosing was without his knowledge too, in which case he had no choice. Listen: I don't know what the Building really is. Dolt may have been right. Perhaps there were originally two sides which, locked in mortal combat, eventually devoured one another. Perhaps, too, this is not a madness of men, but of an organization, an organization that grew too much and one day met a remote offshoot of itself, and began to swallow it up, and swallowed and swallowed, reaching back to itself, back to its own center, and now it loops around and around in an endless swallowing . . . In which case, there need be no other Building, except as a pretense to hide its autophagia . . ."

"What are you?"

"A priest, as you know."

"A priest? You turned me over to Major Erms! You only wear a cassock to hide the uniform!"

"And do you only wear a body to hide the skeleton? Try to understand. I am hiding nothing. You say I betrayed you. But here everything is illusion: betrayal, treason, even omniscience—for omniscience is not only impossible, but quite unnecessary when its counterfeit suffices, a fabrication of stray reports, allusions, words mumbled in one's sleep or retrieved from the latrines . . . It is not omniscience but the faith in it that matters."

Would they or would they not want him to tell me this?

Now grown very pale, he hissed with unexpected vehemence:

"You *still* believe in the Building's wisdom! What else can I say? You've seen the men in command, those deaf, wart-covered sclerotic relics at the top! Look here."

He took a small, smooth stone out of his pocket and showed it to me. It was spotted like a bird's egg.

"Nothing but a stupid piece of gravel! A few spots . . . a little hole here . . . But take a million pieces of gravel like this, a trillion, and an atmosphere will form around them, the wind will blow over them, and cosmic rays will bombard them—until from out a pile of debris there will crawl forth something we call—Sacred . . . And who gave the order? Who? It is exactly the same with the Building . . ."

"You mean, the Building is Nature itself?"

"Heavens, no! They have nothing in common beyond the fact that they are both ineffably perfect. And here you thought you were a prisoner in a labyrinth of evil, where everything was pregnant with meaning, where even the theft of one's instructions was a ritual, that the Building destroyed only in order to build, to build only in order to destroy the more—and you took this for the wisdom of evil . . . Hence your mental somersaults and contortions. You writhed on the hook of your own question mark to solve that equation of horror. But I tell you there is no solution, no equation, no destruction, no instructions, no evil—there is only the Building—only—the Building—"

"Only the Building?" I echoed, my hair on end.

"Only the Building," he echoed my echo, shivering. "This is not wisdom, this is a blind and all-encompassing perfection, a perfection not of man's making but which arose from man, or rather from the community of man. Human evil, you see, is so petty and frail, while here we have something grand and mighty at work . . . An ocean of blood and sweat and urine! One thundering death rattle from a million throats! A great monument of feces, the product of countless generations! Here you can drown in people, choke on them, waste away in a vast wilderness of people! Behold: they will stir their coffee as they calmly tear you to shreds, chat and pick their noses as they outrage your corpse, and brew more coffee as it stiffens, and you will be a hairless, worn-out and abandoned doll, a broken rattle, an old rag yellow and forgotten in the corner . . . That is how perfection operates, not wisdom! Wisdom is you, yourself—or maybe two people! You and someone else, that intimate flash of honesty from eye to eye . . ."

I watched his deathly pale face and wondered where I'd heard all this before, it sounded so familiar. Then I remembered—that sermon, the sermon about choking, evil and the Devil, the sermon which Brother Persuasion told me was intended as provocation . . .

"How can I believe you?" I groaned. He shuddered.

"O sinner!!" he screamed in a whisper. "Dost thou still doubt that what may be a harmless conversation or joke on one level doth constitute, on another, legal action and, on yet another, a battle of wits between Departments? Verily, if thou followest this line of thought, thou shalt end up nowhere, since here anything, hence everything, leadeth everywhere!"

"You've lost me."

"Treason is inevitable. But the Building's purpose is to make treason impossible. Ergo, we must make the inevitable evitable. But how? Obliterate truth. What's treason when truth is but another way of lying? That is why there is no place here for any real action, whether legitimate despair or honest crime—anything genuine will weigh you down, drag you to the bottom for good. Listen! Come in with me! We'll form a secret alliance, a conspiracy of two! This will liberate us!"

"You're mad!"

"No! If we trust one another, we can save ourselves yet. I will restore you to yourself, and you will do the same for me. Only in this way can we be free!"

"They'll arrest us!"

"All the more reason we should work together! Knowing our cause is lost from the start, we will redeem ourselves! I shall die for you and you shall die for me—and they'll never be able to take that truth from us! Think of it! You will be Christ, and I Judas—since I was ordered to incite you to treason as an agent provocateur . . ."

"What are you saying?"

"You *still* don't understand? I'm an *agent provocateur* because I'm a priest. Only as your agent provocateur am I, a priest, allowed to say what I've said here. Of course, we expect you to cooperate . . ."

"How could I possibly cooperate?"

"How could you not? You're obviously at the end of your rope. Today you denounced an innocent man, a man who was on your side, for Dolt was—as far as you knew—on your side when you denounced him. You'll cooperate all right, if not now, then tomorrow, if not with me, then with somebody else. But then, don't you see, you'll be cooperating on the Building's terms, which means cooperating just for appearances. Don't do that! Cooperate here and now, once and for all, heart and soul, so that in the foul bosom of Treachery we may bear witness to the blessed birth of Truth!"

"But then you'll have to inform on me as the man who agreed to join your conspiracy!"

"Of course! And they'll take it as a false conspiracy, a conspiracy entered into only under orders, not realizing that your betrayal is voluntary, from the heart as it were, and so you, knowing this and acting with that knowledge, will fill the dreadful vacuum, and thus our conspiracy, engineered by the Building to be another false conspiracy, will become Flesh. Will you cooperate now?"

I was silent.

"You refuse?" he asked, and a tear rolled down his cheek.

I sat there, my leg still dancing, and I didn't see or hear him any longer. Once again I was surrounded by those endless rows of white corridors and white doors, robbed of everything that could ever be mine. It was with the lifeless light of the labyrinth before me that I said:

"I'll cooperate."

His face lit up. He turned away and dabbed his forehead and cheeks with a handkerchief.

"Now you wonder if I'll *really* betray you," he said at last. "It can't be helped. All promises, vows and oaths are worthless here, so I'll only say this: not today. Also, no recognition signals: they wouldn't help. Our weapon will be openness —we'll make no secret of our conspiracy and they'll never believe us. Now I'll go and denounce you to my superior. Meanwhile, act natural, do whatever you would normally do."

"I should go to the Registry then?"

"Would you otherwise?"

"I guess not."

"Then don't. Get some rest instead, you'll need your strength. Tomorrow, after dinner, between the two marble caryatids near the elevator on the seventh level, Two will be waiting for you."

"Two?"

"That's me. Our code names."

"And I'm One?"

"Right. I'd better leave now. We shouldn't be seen together—it'll look suspicious."

"Wait! What should I say if they interrogate me before we meet again?"

"Whatever you like."

"Can I betray you?"

"Of course. They already know about our conspiracy— the false one, that is, not the true one. As long as you don't begin to—"

He broke off.

"And you too."

"And me too, yes. It's best not to think too much. Just remember: this way we save one another, we redeem ourselves, even if we perish. Farewell."

He left quickly, stirring the air with his departure—a pleasant breeze.

He was off to denounce me—ostensibly. But how did I know it was only ostensibly? Either way, I didn't care. I got up. I had something to say but there was no one around to listen. I coughed deliberately, to hear myself. But the room had no echo. I peeked into the next room—a table and a tape recorder, its spools slowly turning. I took them off, tore the tape into little pieces and stuffed my pockets with them, then headed for the bathroom.

13

The wailing in the pipes woke me up. I opened my eyes and noticed for the first time that the bathroom ceiling had a bas-relief: a scene from paradise. There was Adam and Eve playing hide-and-seek among the trees, and the serpent lurking on a branch, apparently debating whether or not to take a bite out of Eve's plump behind, and there was an angel on a cloud busily writing a denunciation—exactly as Dolt had described it. Dolt! I sat up, wide awake, and realized I was freezing—the towel wrapped around my naked body was no protection against the chill of that tiled floor—I was stiff as a corpse. Only a long, hot bath brought me back to life. Then I looked myself over in the mirror. It was no surprise to find an old man looking back at me. Yesterday had lasted forever, drained me, taken a lifetime . . . if only that idiotic song wouldn't plague me . . .

Hey, the Building, hey!
What makes the Building stay?
The Antibuilding makes it stay!
Hey!

I was singing it even now—I could tell—my lips moved in the mirror! Come to think of it, though, I hadn't really aged. Merely a bad hangover. I must have been dead drunk to have accepted Father Orfini's proposition. A conspiracy—good Lord! And a conspiracy of two!

I sang in the empty bathroom—listened—no one was joining in. I was accustomed to eating at odd hours—on the other hand, I wasn't hungry after last night (night?)—so I gargled a little and left.

At the elevator I realized I wasn't my old self—I mean, where was I going anyway? Peace and quiet, that's what I needed. The smartest thing would be to join a crowd and follow it to some big meeting or assembly. There I could collect my thoughts without standing out—and get away from the bathroom and this hateful isolation!

But there was no crowd, only an occasional officer—and one can't follow an occasional officer very well. I wandered up and down the fifth level, then the sixth, took an elevator to the eighth where I seemed to recall the doors along one corridor, indicating the presence of a large hall on the other side. Today the corridor was empty. I waited around for a while. No one showed up. I went in.

The anteroom of a large museum. Along the highly polished parquet stood a row of long showcases that blazed light in the general gloom. The lane between them ended in a turn, but the reflection on the dark walls there indicated more of the same around the turn. On display were hands—hands severed at the wrist, often clasped in pairs on their glass shelves, very true-to-life hands, too true-to-life—not only was the skin dull and the fingernails shiny, but there were even little hairs on the backs. Frozen in an incredible number of poses, they seemed caught forever in roles of a vast drama, a theater under glass. I decided to go through the entire collection. Why not? I had plenty of time to kill. I passed: the hands of a saint (praying) and the hands of a sinner (dealing cards); fists of anger, fists of despair, and triumphant fists; then challenging hands and hands of denial; senile fingers giving a shaky blessing, senile fingers begging for bread; then some indecent gestures; over here, the shy blossoming of sweet innocence in the shadow of doom, and over there, a mother's relentless concern. I followed the turn and walked on, then stopped to take in one particularly heartwarming scene—enacted by the most eloquent gesture imaginable—but found it a bit too cloying and so moved on. The connoisseur awoke within me. Now I could appraise an expression at a glance—this was shallow, that a trifle overdone, and so on—and soon grew weary and bored, began looking for more complex, more subtle presentations, and quickly found that the creators of this exhibit had the very same idea—around the next turn, the gestures were more and more controlled, laconic, enigmatic . . . ambiguous . . .

No waving of fists here, no rude insistence—the maudlin twist of fingers breathed foul play, for that rosy enclosure shielded not a bright (imaginary) candle but, crouched furtively there in the palm, the little finger, the pinkie, and where did the pinkie point? My interest was rekindled. I savored, like vintage wine, the way one finger suddenly side-stepped the monastic solemnity of its fellows and signaled to someone behind my back—deceit and deception indeed permeated the digital air, that patted and pointed space from shelf to shelf, for one gesture negated another nearby or across the way, and a forest of fingers clamored at the glass or gathered in the shadows to connive among many thumbs . . . Here a plump knuckle frolicked and cut capers, and there were handsprings, handstands, but suddenly in the midst of their innocent abandon a hangnail passed across a wrist, all thumbs turned down, and accusingly they pointed—they pointed—they pointed at me!!

I started to run—hundreds of hands, high and low against the glass like a swarm of spiders or white, twisted worms rushing by—"But why so many?" I thought—"What can it mean—can it mean—what kind of museum—?—I'd better leave—"

Someone came running out of the darkness straight at me, the shadows flashing across his face, the mouth open in a voiceless scream and the eyes blank—but I was able to stop at the last minute, and reached out and touched the cold, smooth surface of—a mirror.

I stood before it, and behind me in the dark, blurry, many-aquariumed depths, in the silent, lifeless sea of a thousand groping signs, revolting mimes, there hung the numb and bloody hands of madness. I pressed my forehead to the cold glass, afraid to look.

The mirror moved, gave way, opened—the surface of a door—and I was in a tiny room, practically a closet. A little man, a very little man, sat behind a table in a trench coat and, bending over (nearsighted?), filed his nails.

"Have a seat," he said, not looking up. "Chair's in the corner. Remove the towel first. Have trouble seeing? It'll pass. Wait a while."

"I'm in a hurry," I said. "How do I get out of here?"

"In a hurry? Better take a seat, catch your breath. There's pen and paper here."

"What?"

He filed his nails in a fury.

"Go ahead, I won't bother you."

"I have no intention of writing anything. How do I get out of here?"

"You have no intention?"

He stopped in mid-file and gave me a watery look. I'd seen him before, though I hadn't really—red hair, thin mustache, hardly any chin, wrinkled jowls, as if there were walnuts stored inside.

"Then *I'll* write," he offered, returning to his nails, "and all you have to do is sign it."

"Sign what?"

"A little confession."

"So that's your game!" I thought, careful not to clench my teeth—clenching my teeth could give me away.

"I don't know what you mean," I said stiffly.

"Ah? Surely you haven't forgotten your little party? . . ."

I said nothing. He blew on his nails, rubbed them on the lapel of his coat, looked them over carefully, then pulled a thick, black volume out of a drawer, opened it and read:

"Whosoever disseminates, circulates, advocates, or in any way promulgates and propagates the notion that the Antibuilding does not exist, is subject under Paragraph Two to immediate exoclasis—without appeal." He smiled coaxingly. "Well?"

"I'm innocent."

"Of course you're innocent! Why, you were only sipping cognac and listening. A man can't help listening, can he?

We weren't born with ear flaps, were we? Unfortunately, the law is not so understanding . . ."

He opened the book to another page.

"Whosoever witnesses or learns of an offense as specified under Paragraph N Section N and fails to report it to the appropriate division within N hours of its perpetration is held liable and subject to summary epistoclasis—unless the Court finds mitigating circumstances as outlined under Paragraph n, small n."

He put the volume away and watched me with his watery eyes for some time, then moved his lips:

"A little confession?"

I shook my head.

"Well then," he coaxed, not discouraged, "a wee bit of a confession?"

"I have nothing to confess."

"An infinitesimal confession?"

"No!" I yelled, furious. He blinked like a startled bird.

"No?"

"No."

"Not even yes?"

"No."

"Look, I'll help you. For example: 'present at a party thrown by Professors X, Y and Z on such and such a day and hour et cetera and so on, I was made an unwilling witness of this, that, and the other.'—Well?"

"I refuse to make any such report."

He stared at me with the wide, round eyes of a chicken.

"Am I under arrest?" I asked.

"Troublemaker," he said and blinked again. "Let's try something else, shall we? Here boy! Fetch! Roll over! Confess!"

"Stop it!"

"Or free association. Spy? Price? Conspire? Piracy? Perspire! Conspiracy!"

I was silent.

"Still no?"

He jumped up on the table, as if ready to hurl himself at me.

"Perhaps *this* will refresh the Count's memory!"

And he held out a round box full of small black buttons.

"Oh," I gasped. He jumped down and made a note of it, mumbling to himself: "Admits he knows Orfini . . ."

"I didn't say that!"

"Oh?" he said with a wink. "Just *O* then? *O* as in zero, naught? Nothing more? A poor, homeless *O?* Come now, let's give it a friend, a nice little *r . . . f . . .* Can't you guess? A man of the cloth . . . Cross and double-cross . . ."

"No," I said.

"No *O,*" he added. "Oh No."

He was clearly enjoying himself. I decided to maintain a stony silence.

"Or how about a song?" he suggested. " 'Rub-a-dub-dub, two men in a tub . . .' No? Do you know this one?—'Hey, the Building, hey!' "

He waited.

"A tough nut to crack," he said at last, inspecting the black buttons. "Tough and rough and full of bluff. Wants a Grand Inquisitor—Torquemada—Pontius Pilate. *Ecce homo!* What a shame! We're fresh out of crosses around here—no nails, no thorns, no spear in the side—sorry! Only the boss gets a little cross . . ."

He took to filing his nails again, and after a while grumbled:

"Please leave."

"I can go?" I asked, amazed.

He ignored me. I looked around for the door—there it was, and it was even open. Why hadn't I noticed it before? At the doorway I looked back—he was completely absorbed in his nails. Outside was a large, cold corridor. After walking some distance, I became aware of something heavy at my sides, attached and swinging like buckets of water. I stopped and looked down—my hands, incredibly swollen and dripping sweat—"Oh," I thought. But why Oh? Why not Ah? I didn't have to oh, I could have ahhed—ah, what a bastard I was! A regular bastard—but why regular—regulation—when I could be an uncommon bastard, bastard with a capital *B, B* as in bomb and boom?!

Door, elevator, corridor, door, elevator again, sweetly descending and how nice it is when old friends get together for a little third degree. I took a deep breath. Relief. Peace. No conspiracy, not a trace.

I was a Bastard, proud but still a little bashful.

And out the elevator—which level this? It mattered not. Take any door and turn the knob—

A pink room with plaster pilasters, paintings on the walls, flat Rembrandt-brown portraits in tulle and lace, and seated beneath the largest—a pretty girl, sweet sixteen and scared. I waited for her to speak—she didn't—not bad —not bad—a bright face, golden bangs, the dark violet eyes of a distrusting child, full red lips, a schoolgirl's dress with short sleeves and the nipples poking through, defiant. And the legs, the pink heels—the sandals had slipped off beneath my gaze—and those helpless little hands! "Ah," I thought, "so white . . ." White? Wait! Ah! Lily white—the spy in the bathroom—on the agenda! The doctor, the plates, and now lily white . . .

She looked at me unblinking with her violet eyes, and I looked at her naked neck, so naked beneath that dark painting—a song in the night—not a bad metaphor either —I took a step toward her, a villainous step, I stabbed her with my eyes, and the quiescence of her flesh filled me with exquisite terror as I took another step and watched each nipple ticktock—ticktock—ticktock in time with the hammering heart. A frozen moment: The Rake's Progress.

Another step—the knees touched—her head went back, seeking sanctuary in its mass of golden hair. I bent over. A slight tremble of the lips—the arms lay helpless—now I should deflower her—she expected no less—what else could I do under the circumstances? But perhaps she wasn't really a little girl to be deflowered, perhaps she was the block where I would have to lay my head and make my last confession and await the ax. Why was she here, anyway?

"On the other hand," I thought, peering into her golden lashes, "I'm here too and I'm innocent, so why shouldn't she be innocent?" Was there no end to this analyzing, agonizing, temporizing? A man could go mad! Rape and be done with it!

Easy to say, not so easy to put into operation. A kiss was the obvious place to start—our breaths already mingled—but a kiss as a prelude to defloration—it wasn't right, wasn't right because, even in the most contrived and underhanded kiss lay something—something right—too right. A kiss was a sign, a symbol, an emblem, an allegory, and I was through with such games—I wanted to trample on her lily whiteness unequivocally, without qualification or reservation—for what is an outrage if it isn't an outrage?

Forget the kiss then—and my hovering over her maiden modesty was false—a pose—"Better carry her off in my arms," I decided, stepping back—a serious mistake—it looked too much like a retreat, vacillation—and where could I take her? There was only the armchair—other than the hard floor—and picking her up and throwing her back in the same chair would be ridiculous—an outrage cannot be ridiculous and be an outrage.

Then seize her with shameless brutality! The armchair was too low—so I kneeled—another mistake! This was a posture of humility, obedience—the noble knight requesting his lady's favor before the fray. One could not violate one on bended knee—and violate I had to, and quickly, before she started to bawl—then we would have a sniveling brat on our hands and no more lily white!

Up her skirt, then? A ticklish business—what if she starts giggling—not as a virgin—but because it tickles? No lily white, no outrage—only a tickle and a giggle——? God in heaven!!

This was his work—that interrogator—he planted her here—*ex ungue leonem*—in that case, no going up her skirt, nothing underhanded, undercover—but bold, head-on action—bull by the horns—a frontal kiss, an all-out blitz-kiss—lightning and thunder, fire and brimstone, eye to eye and tooth to tooth! Passion!! Lust!! I swooped down —something was wrong—her mouth was full—white —a whiff of—of—what? Cheese! Cream cheese!!

Slowly, I got to my feet and brushed off my knees. That was that. Lily white—snow white—cream cheese——

On my way out I looked back: relieved, she resumed her chewing, brought her sandwich out of hiding. She hid it so it would be easier for me to——God in heaven!

I shut the door behind me and went quietly on my way, thinking of bastards. A shot rang out—nearby. I turned around, not in the mood for trouble—I had enough of my own—when I noticed three officers standing in front of a door with a cushion. I understood.

There were essentially two kinds of shooting. One, usually after breakfast, came in a deafening barrage—gunfire, screams, curses, ricocheting bullets, falling plaster. Those corridor battles were executed in great haste, ending with the coded groans of the dying and bells signifying the approach of the theologicals. On occasion, when elevator doors would accidentally open, you might see a corpse or two come tumbling down the empty shaft from some upper level—that's how they got rid of them. But this was a single shot—and they were usually preceded by a small procession, no more than two or three officers carrying a revolver on a velvet cushion. They would enter an office, return without the revolver and wait at the door—a high-ranking officer got tassels on his cushion. Then the body would be removed during lunch, when no one was around to gawk.

Fifteen minutes before my rendezvous with the Judas priest. But why bother now? I had to think. Our conspiracy was not only known and tolerated, but ordered—the false conspiracy, that is. But beneath the falsehood we tried to build the truth. If I didn't show up, it would look

like I was afraid—and they might guess that I *was* afraid
—so I had to go.

My sense of shame began to pass. I paced a quiet corridor between two bathrooms. I wanted so desperately to
justify myself—I hit upon a thought, a hopelessly naïve
but tempting thought—could this be a dream, an unusually
persistent and perverse dream? Then even if I couldn't wake
up at once (the dream seemed too powerful for that), at
least I would know, from now until it ended, that I wasn't
responsible. I stopped in front of a white wall, looked
around to see that no one was coming, and focused my will
on it—to soften it—such things usually work in dreams,
even the worst nightmares. But it didn't work—the wall was
as hard as ever. Another possibility—I was in someone
else's dream—in which case, of course, the dreamer would
have more control over the wall than I . . .

Impossible to prove, either way. I went back to the main
corridor and took an elevator up to meet the priest. Why
that lily white? Apparently to show me that even a Bastard
couldn't—couldn't defy the Building. I could almost see
that little interrogator now, wagging his finger at me in
playful reproach—playful, like dead men dancing on air
at the scaffold——

The elevator went up and up, the numbers jumped, the
contacts clicked, the milky light dimmed and brightened,
and suddenly I saw him—really saw him—through the
crack in the door as the elevator climbed. He stood there
in his trench coat, lost in thought—did he see me or not?

The elevator was slowing down. Through the crack I
saw a pair of polished shoes, then a black coat, a row of
buttons—a cassock! The priest! He was waiting for me,
right at the door! The elevator jerked to a stop—but I
pressed a button and sent it back down—not that I suspected treachery—I didn't suspect treachery—but the
pleasant motion of descending made me feel secure. Again
the contacts clicked, the milky light brightened and dimmed
—my small, cozy room was falling softly through the

Building—at the bottom I pushed a button and went up again . . .

Levels passed, blank walls, floors, a pair of legs, a ceiling, another floor—and again the little interrogator in the trench coat waiting patiently for an elevator—and more walls, a curtain of stone lowered over the scene . . .

I held my breath—the eighth level was next, and the priest again, feet first, still waiting for me—so down again —the interrogator again—I watched them carefully from my hiding place, one at a time, a biologist taking samples.

Each, one at a time, stood casually, concertedly unconcerned—but I, able to jump from level to level and face to face, could see—to my horror—the composite: the interrogator's upper lip and the priest's lower lip made a smile, a smile spread over several levels—yet neither, singly, smiled—it was the *Building* that smiled! At the bottom I jumped out and ran off, followed only by an angry buzzing —they were buzzing for the elevator on all the levels now —but I was far away and free of them——

So the priest did betray me, as I expected—that required some thought—but—but wasn't this the bottom level?

Somewhere—nearby—was the legendary Gate—an exit from the Building.

Everything was different here, very different. I wasn't walking down a corridor now but through a high and spacious hall—columns on every side, footsteps in the distance—receding—a crowd would have been more comfortable—I felt terribly conspicuous, particularly since I intended to escape. Escape was the only thing left. Why hadn't I escaped before? Escaped instead of struggling with the Mission, the instructions—the false instructions—and the false conspiracy which turned out to be genuinely false. Why? Fear? I did fear the guards—they might question me, demand to see my pass—but I hadn't even considered the possibility of escape. Why? Because I had nowhere to go, nothing to return to? Because the Building could reach me anywhere? Or was it because, in spite of all the torment

I'd endured—against, entirely against, my better knowledge—I still held on to my faith—like a last hope, a hope against hope—in that accursed, that thrice accursed Mission of mine??

There was the Gate up ahead. Open and—God in heaven!—unguarded! Between two towering pillars at the end of a mighty hall—the nave of a great cathedral—dead silence, not even an echo—and then I saw him.

This was the second guard I'd seen in the Building. Like the first, the one who guarded a death, he was stiff and straight, had white gloves and a gun, denying his own existence with that lifeless stare—not a person, but an object of the Building.

The Gate was ajar, streaming white light—if I ran for it, would he shoot? Let him shoot! No more deliberations, no more fears and hopes—both deceiving—and no more honor or dishonor—loyalty, treachery—no more!!

I walked up to the guard. He looked through me—as if I weren't there—and now the door—and the sunlight!

Six steps to the Gate. I stopped.

The spy in the bathroom was waiting for me. I promised him I'd come. Of course, he was as much a Judas as the rest, he made no secret of it. Yet how can one betray a traitor?

He had warned me about the doctor, the plates, the girl— he *knew*. In that case, he knew I would escape, that I would never be coming back. Then how could he ask me to come back, make me promise to come back? How could he count on it? What did he know?

I had to take care of this unfinished business first. Then my escape would be more than an escape—it would be a challenge, a challenge to the Building itself, for though I could be as deceitful and as false as It, instead I would be forgiving, virtuous, magnanimous, beneficent...

I turned around, passed the rigid guard again, went back through the hall to the elevator—this one was a luxury model, all in red—the mechanism hummed sweetly as I pushed the button and we lifted up, contacts clicking, and sailed into the many-leveled space of the Building.

The corridor, an old friend, white and shining with its long rows of doors, led me past officers with briefcases, officers without briefcases, gray officers, thin officers, and that last officer just before the bathroom, fat and jolly— panting beneath his large stack of papers as he hurried by——

I shut the door behind me. The place seemed empty— except for a steady tapping, persistent and distinct, and disturbing in the silence. A faucet dripping.

I sighed, took a few steps in, was about to call out for him—and froze.

He was lying in the tub, the tub was full, he was naked and his throat was slit, like a pig. The hair was plastered down like a helmet, silver on the sides, the head was turned away and faced the wall, and the face was underwater. A fist still gripped the razor. Blood trickled from that hideous wound and mixed with the water in dark whorls and spirals.

I came closer. The face was still hidden from view, as if he had shied away at the last moment, or didn't want to look at the razor. Or was hiding from the moment when I would find him.

He had to do it, of course. This was absolutely the only way to convince me that he hadn't lied. Words, entreaties, threats wouldn't have helped. He was presenting me with the one irrefutable proof.

I looked around. The clothes lay under the sink, carefully folded. Apparently he hadn't wished to bloody them. Had he left some sign, some message, a last will and testament, or a warning—anything written—I would have my doubts again. This he knew, and so left only a naked body, as if to say by the very nakedness of death that not everything was false, that there was, in the final analysis, something absolute and unmistakable, something that no amount of subterfuge could ever alter.

He died, then, for my sake—and so doing, saved himself.

Cautiously, I leaned over the tub. Why had he turned away at the crucial moment? Large drops gathered at the mouth of the faucet and hit the red water in shuddering slaps. I had to make sure. I tried to lift him by the shoulders —he rolled like a log, rolled face up, water streaming off in tears, droplets trembling on his bristly chin. I had to make sure. The razor? I couldn't pry it from his icy fist. Why not? Shouldn't the fingers loosen when the heart has beaten its last? Why wouldn't he let go? And the tears, why were they false? Why did he lie in precisely *that* position? Why did he hide his face? And why—why did the pipes whine and shriek and sing—?

"Give me the razor!" I screamed. "Traitor! Bastard! Give me the razor!!"